New School, New Rules

Book
One

Iggy the Iguana
New School New Rules

Melissa M. Williams
Illustrated by Kelley Ryan

LongTale PUBLISHING

New School, New Rules

Copyright © 2015 by Melissa M. Williams

For information address Long Tale Publishing,
6824 Long Drive, Houston, TX 77087

Library of Congress Control Number: 2014917586
ISBN 978-1-941515-58-7 (Hardback)

JUVENILE FICTION / Animals / Reptiles

Illustrations by Kelley Ryan

Design by Monica Thomas for TLC Graphics
www.TLCGraphics.com

In-house Editor: Sharon Wilkerson

www.IggytheIguana.com

Table of Contents

The Jitters

Iggy stared out the kitchen window trying to think of an excuse not to go to school. Even the smell of his favorite breakfast made his stomach turn. He pushed his scrambled eggs away and sighed.

"What's wrong, son? Aren't you feeling well?" asked his mother, while using both of her hands to spike up the spines on his head.

Iggy squirmed. He preferred to fix his own spines. "Mom, what if I'm the only iguana in my class?"

Mrs. Green looked at him with a sympathetic smile. "It's natural to be nervous on your first day at a new school," she said and poured orange juice into Iggy's glass.

"But what if everyone's bigger than me? What if I'm allergic to furry animals?" Iggy took a sip of his juice, but even that didn't taste good to him.

"Sweetie, you can't go to an all-lizard school forever."

"Why not?" Iggy set down his glass and pushed that away too.

"Because, it's time for you to meet animals who are different than you. You'll be fine. You'll make friends in no time. Now try to eat some breakfast."

Iggy had attended the same private elementary school all his life in a suburban area of Houston. He never had to worry about making new friends because he attended school with the same twelve lizards ever since Pre-K. Iggy considered this group of lizards to be more like family than friends. The idea of making new friends was terrifying for the reserved iguana.

"At least I don't have to wear a uniform," Iggy said while looking down at his new plaid shorts. He began to take a bite of his eggs just as the back door swung wide open. Iggy perked up at the sight of his dad bouncing in with a huge, open-mouthed smile on his face.

"Good morning Champ," said his dad. "Ready for school?"

Iggy cringed at the word, *school*. "Hi Dad, how was your run?"

"It was nice and humid. Mosquitoes everywhere." Iggy could tell his dad was being sarcastic. Iguanas preferred drier climates and no one likes mosquitoes.

"I can't complain. I can take the Houston humidity and bugs to get to run on these flat trails any day." Mr. Green was a professional runner. Iguanas are known for their speed and great running legs. He trained nearby at Memorial Park and coached other runners. The Green family had just moved into the city so that he could be closer to the training grounds, forcing Iggy and his little sister, Molly, to have to start a new school.

Iggy's nerves had almost gone away until his mom walked over to the table and said, "I bet your dad was nervous on the day of his first race." She handed her husband a glass of water.

"I'll say! Nervous and excited at the same time," Mr. Green said and gulped down his water.

"I'm just nervous, Dad."

As Mr. Green pulled out his chair, a little lizard in a pink tutu darted across the kitchen and sat down next to Iggy. He rolled his eyes at his little sister, hoping his mom would not allow her to wear a dance tutu and princess crown to school.

"Why are you nervous, Iggy?" Molly asked and took a sip of her brother's orange juice.

Iggy grabbed the glass out of her hand. "I'm not nervous," he said defensively. He knew Molly wouldn't understand. She talked to everyone, even her stuffed animals.

Mr. Green patted Molly on the head and sat down. "Well, of course you're going to be a little skittish. It's called the fear of the unknown."

"Fear of the unknown?" Iggy questioned. It sounded like his dad was talking about a mission to space, not fourth grade. Dad's words just weren't helping this time. Iggy turned back to his plate of food and managed to take a few bites.

After breakfast, Mrs. Green drove Iggy and Molly to school, which was right down the street. "Just be yourself, honey." Mrs. Green kissed Iggy good-bye in front of Memorial Elementary.

Iggy slowly crept up to the school's entrance and pulled back the heavy wooden door. Standing in the doorframe, he looked around, noticing the building was much larger than his old school. The ceiling went up forever. Just as Iggy crept forward the heavy door slammed shut on his long tail. "Ouch!" he yelled. He turned around, trying to pull his tail loose before someone noticed him.

"Are you okay?" asked a voice nearby.

Great a witness. Iggy slowly turned his head to see a beautiful lime green and tan lizard.

"Hi," she said. "I'm Lizibeth. I know how that feels!" She swung her own cute and dainty tail around.

Iggy was a bit tongue-tied as he searched for

something to say back. "That wasn't my first time doing that," he stuttered. "Oh, um... I'm Iggy."

"Whoa! Your tail is sooo long!" Lizibeth gasped, as she looked down to see if his tail was hurt.

Iggy self-consciously pulled his tail close to his body, trying to hide its length. "I hate dragging this useless thing around."

"I hear ya," laughed Lizibeth. "So what grade are you in?"

"Me? Um…" he said and paused. "Fourth."

"Me too," she said and smiled.

Iggy quickly added, "And today's my first day at this school."

Lizibeth tried to put the fidgety iguana at ease. "Oh, you'll love it here. Everyone's nice!"

As Iggy looked around, he pointed at the clock on the wall. "We don't want to be late on the first day of school and all."

"It's okay, we don't have far to go," Lizibeth reassured him.

Both lizards started walking toward the fourth grade classroom. Iggy couldn't believe the first animal he met was actually a lizard. It was nice to have something in common. Hopefully the rest of the kids would be just as friendly.

I'm Changing Colors Again!

The two reptiles approached the door to the classroom. Iggy's mouth dropped to the ground when he spotted the creature standing in the middle of the room. He had never seen such an animal. He kind of looked like a reptile, and yet like an amphibian, too...possibly a frog, but not smooth like a frog. He looked more like a toad, but with horns. The enormous toad had horns and spikes all over his body. He even had three tall horns on the top of his head!

"He looks mean," Lizibeth whispered in Iggy's ear.

"Is that lizard our teacher?" Iggy whispered back.

"I don't think he's a lizard," responded Lizibeth.

"Then what is he?" Iggy asked.

"Come on in children. Don't just stand there with your mouths on the floor," the horned toad said in a stern tone. "Find your name on your desk and have a seat," he grunted.

The desks were sectioned off in groups of four. Iggy scurried around the room, looking down for his name

until he bumped heads with Lizibeth. Their desks were in the same group and right next to each other.

"Ouch!" she squeaked.

"Sorry, are you okay?"

"Yeah, I guess we're both a little clumsy, huh?" she said, rubbing her forehead.

Iggy looked down to the ground realizing Lizibeth had already picked up on his klutziness.

"You can call me Liz…all my friends do."

Iggy felt a wave of heat rushing to his cheeks as he started to blush. He quickly took his seat across from a quiet, brown box turtle. The turtle looked up at Iggy and gave him a head nod. Iggy noticed he was drawing waves on the outside of his folder. Iggy nodded back and decided to speak up. "What's your name?" he asked hesitantly.

The turtle looked up from his artwork. "Hey man, I'm Snap. Snap Shell." The turtle spoke with a surfer accent that Iggy never expected. Iggy was used to hearing more of a country twang from being around Texas lizards all his life.

"Cool, I'm Iggy." The lizard tried to match the turtle's laid-back tone. "So, where ya from, Snap?"

"Here and there. I lived off the coast for a year."

Iggy noticed the puka shells around the turtle's neck. "California? Cool!"

"Nah man, just Galveston."

"Oh," Iggy replied with a bit of disappointment.

"I mean, it's no Cali beach man, but the ocean's the ocean. It's all about the spirit of the wave dude."

Iggy nodded his head, pretending that he understood. He had been to Galveston with his family but wasn't that impressed with all the seaweed and jellyfish washed up on the beachfront.

"Hi Snap," Liz whispered from across her desk.

"Hey, Liz," the box turtle said with a smile. "Man, I wonder if this horned dude is as mean as he looks," Snap whispered.

"Yeah, I don't remember him from last year," Liz said.

18

As the reptiles continued their discussion, more animals started coming into the classroom. Iggy was amazed to see the variety. There were a couple of puppies, a monkey, a pig, a rabbit, a snake, a crab... and then out of nowhere, a big black cat plopped down across the table from Liz.

"Who's the new guy?" the cat asked.

"That's Iggy," Snap said.

Iggy did a quick wave to the cat.

The cat stood back up and held out his paw. "Kit Kat's the name. Kit Kat Kay Kat, and that's cat with a *K*." Kit Kat was a confident fellow with a lot of long black hair... and a bit chubby.

"Nice to meet you," Iggy said.

Everyone's introductions were cut short when the horned toad marched his way to the front of the class. "NOW CLASS!" he boomed. "I am your new principal, Mr. Horn."

19

What? The principal? Iggy gulped. Is this normal? He looked over, stunned to see Kit Kat's hand already raised.

"Yes, what is it?" The principal looked down at Kit Kat with an annoyed look in his eyes.

"So where's our teacher?" asked the curious cat.

"I was getting to that," Principal Horn said and looked the cat up and down. "What's your name, lad?" he asked sternly.

"Kit Kat Kay Kat, with a *K*," Kit Kat answered, sitting straight up in his chair.

"How nice." Mr. Horn crinkled his brow. "Anyhow, your teacher, Mrs. Buff, had a personal emergency and will be back tomorrow. I will be your substitute for today. Now get out a sheet of paper for your morning work," Mr. Horn instructed the class then continued talking as he marched back to his desk. "Fourth grade is a big year for testing, so we will start now."

"Testing?" Iggy questioned.

"Morning work?" Kit Kit whispered. "Hopefully this isn't any everyday thing."

Iggy never had to do morning work at his old school. They usually had time to draw or write stories. Iggy hoped his real teacher wasn't so boring. He seriously felt like crawling under a rock. He started to imagine laying on a nice, hot rock...on the beach...sand in between his long toes. He could hear the waves crashing on the shore when his daydream was interrupted by a dark shadow coming from behind him. He gulped and jumped when an enormous hand landed on his shoulder. He turned around at the sound of Principal Horn breathing deeply though his nose.

"Did you miss the prompt?"

Iggy looked around to see everyone already writing. "What's a prompt?" Iggy accidentally asked out loud.

"Ask your neighbor," the horned toad grunted.

Liz whispered, "Iggy, write about what you did this summer."

"Thanks," he said and bit his lip.

As the class wrote about their summer vacations, Principal Horn slowly paced around the room.

Just as Iggy finished his last sentence, Mr. Horn commanded, "PENCILS DOWN!" He looked around the room and met eyes with Iggy. "You will be first."

"Me? First for what?" Iggy froze. He could feel his cheeks getting hot. He could tell that he was changing colors. He took in a gulp of air as his entire body started to take on a shade of crimson red.

"Whoa!" Kit Kat was the first to notice.

"Don't look so nervous, lad," Principal Horn said with a smug look on his face. "Just read your story to the class."

"Um, in front of everyone?" Iggy gulped. Iggy loved to write, but he dreaded speaking in front of others.

"Yes, and we don't have all day."

Iggy jumped out of his seat, hitting Liz in the lip with his tail.

"Please be careful with that thing!" Principal Horn said glaring at Iggy's tail. Kit Kat let out a laugh.

"Sorry," Iggy squeaked and walked to the front of the class. Iggy's hands trembled. He could barely get out the words, *My Summer Vacation.*

"A little louder," Principal Horn said.

Iggy looked at the class staring back at him. The guinea pig in the desk directly in front of him started to cross her eyes. Iggy looked down to avoid eye contact and quickly remembered an old trick that his dad taught him for stage fright. He pictured everyone in the class sitting in their underwear...except Principal Horn.

"This year, it was my turn to pick where my family should go. My little sister, Molly, wanted to go to a castle in Europe because she thinks she's a princess." Iggy noticed his friends at the table start to giggle. "No, seriously, she wears a crown and a gown, it's soooo...."

"Is this part of your story? Please stay on task," Principal Horn honked.

"Sorry. *I thought castles and fairies would be boring, so I picked Jamaica. I got to surf, parasail and swim with dolphins."* Iggy's paper had finally stopped shaking. *"My whole family went snorkeling, and Molly had to wear floaties because she can't swim. She pouted the whole time. I loved the beach, and I can't wait to go back! The End."*

Kit Kat clapped, and the rest of the class eventually followed. Iggy wasn't sure if he should sit down or take a bow.

"What is the lesson learned?" Mr. Horn asked just as Iggy picked up his foot to move.

Iggy froze. He didn't know he was supposed to add a lesson. Mr. Horn asked him to just write about his summer. "Um. I don't know," Iggy said.

"There's always a lesson. Think lad."

"Maybe the lesson is it's fun to spend time with family?" Iggy questioned his own answer.

"Exactly. Family time is important. Let this be a lesson to us all," Mr. Horn said. "Now be sure to elaborate on that next time. Overall, nice job."

Kit Kat snickered, "That's not what the story was about."

Iggy agreed with Kit Kat. He had pulled that answer out of thin air. Mr. Horn had a way of keeping everyone on their toes. After a few more students read their stories, the morning lessons turned to math and science, and the afternoon came faster than Iggy expected. There was so much more to do in the fourth grade at Memorial than he ever remembered having to do back in third grade.

By the time the school day was over, Iggy was actually looking forward to coming back to school the next day. As he and the rest of his table packed up to go home, Snap asked, "Hey, would you and Liz like to come over to my house to hang out after school tomorrow?"

"Really? Cool, I'll ask my mom tonight," Iggy said.

"Me too!" Liz chimed in.

"Hey, what about me?" Kit Kat jumped into the conversation.

"Of course, dude, the more the merrier."

"Sorry...can't. I've got a hair cut tomorrow after school," the cat informed them as he took off to find his ride.

"That guy does have a lot of hair," Iggy said while rubbing his scaly arm.

The animals walked outside together. Iggy spotted his mom and Molly waiting at the end of the sidewalk.

"Hey you guys, look!" Snap pointed in Molly's direction. "Who's that?"

"You've got to be kidding me," Iggy said under his breath. Molly was wearing a veil, her pink tutu and carrying a bouquet of flowers. Iggy rolled his eyes. *How embarrassing,* he thought to himself. "I'll

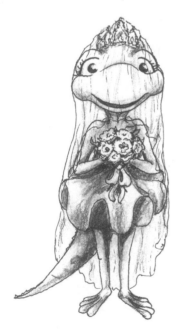

see you guys tomorrow." Iggy quickly walked away, hoping he wouldn't have to explain his little sister. "Nice net." Iggy lifted up the fabric on top of Molly's head. She must have made the costume in kindergarten.

"It's a veil! I'm getting married in the morning.

Here's your invitation. Don't be late!" Molly handed Iggy a piece of pink construction paper with a flower petal glued to the outside.

"It's still wet, Molly!" Iggy groaned as he wiped his hand on the side of a tree. "Aren't you a little young to be getting married?"

"Fine!" The little lizard spun around, causing her veil to fly off her head. The veil floated back and forth in the air, eventually landing in the middle of the street.

"My veil!" Molly screamed. Mrs. Green had to hold her back so she wouldn't run into the street.

"I'll go get it." Iggy looked both ways, just as a monkey on a scooter ran over it.

"No! Someone catch that monkey!" Molly screamed and reached out the hand her mom wasn't holding.

Iggy walked out into the street, shaking his head. He was used to Molly's drama, but he looked around to see if any of his friends had seen her ridiculous performance. Iggy picked up the veil and returned to the curb.

"There's a tire mark on it," Molly cried, nearly ripping the veil out of Iggy's hand.

"We'll clean it at home," her mom said. "How was your first day of school, honey?" Mrs. Green looked at Iggy.

He was quick to answer. "Way better than I thought. I already have three really good friends. Can I hang out at Snap Shell's house with Liz tomorrow? It's right down the street."

"That should be okay. I will need his parents' phone number."

"Awesome!" On the way home, Iggy was pretty sure his butterflies were gone for good. He couldn't wait for school tomorrow. Maybe his mom and dad were right.

Just Take Off
Your Shell

The next day, Iggy couldn't keep his eyes off the clock. He had gotten permission to play for one hour after school at Snap's house. As soon as the bell rang, Iggy, Liz and Snap jumped out of their seats and headed straight toward the lockers.

"Bye, Mrs. Buff!" Iggy waved to his new fourth grade teacher.

"See you tomorrow, Iggy." The grey terrier said good-bye to each of her students as they exited her class.

The reptiles walked excitedly all the way to Snap's house. On the walk home, they wasted no time discussing what they thought about their new teacher, Mrs. Buff.

29

"Mrs. Buff is definitely nicer than Principal Horn," said Snap.

"He wasn't so bad," Iggy said. "I bet Mrs. Buff is a grandma, though."

"She's got some grey hair," agreed Liz. "I wonder what the emergency situation was yesterday?"

"She probably had to go to the doctor. Grandmas always have to go to the doctor," said Snap.

As Liz and Iggy continued talking, they suddenly noticed Snap was missing. "Can you long-legged lizards slow down?" the box shell yelled from behind.

"Oh, no! Sorry, Snap." Iggy looked back to see the turtle with his tongue hanging out of his mouth, gasping for air. "Why don't you take off that shell? It looks like it's slowing you down."

"Very funny. Turtles can't just take off their shells, man." Snap Shell caught up to the lizards, and Liz giggled at Iggy's remark.

"But don't you change it... switch it out?"

"You're not kidding, are you? Haven't you ever met a turtle before?"

"Uh, not face to face." Iggy felt silly that he didn't know more about turtles or any other animal for that matter. "Only lizards went to my old school," Iggy informed Snap.

"That's weird. Were other animals not allowed?" Snap asked.

"No, that's not it. It was just a really small school for all the lizards in my old neighborhood."

"I see. Well, mostly turtles lived in Galveston. Seagulls too. Man those guys are loud and poop a lot."

"That's disgusting!" Liz screeched.

"It's really disgusting if you step in it." Snap laughed.

"Gross!" Iggy and Liz yelled together.

As the three reptiles approached the turtle's house, they could see the back of a big box shell turtle. Iggy recognized the pattern on the back of the shell. It was identical to Snap's. The turtle turned around, and Iggy could see he had a rag and spray bottle in his hand.

"Pops is washing the windows again. He washes them everyday," Snap said and opened the door. The lizards followed him into the kitchen. Iggy noticed the house was exceptionally clean. There was a bowl of carrot and celery sticks on the table.

"Yummy! Carrot sticks are my favorite," Liz said and reached for a snack.

"My pops tries to put out a healthy snack after school," explained the turtle. "It looks like today we are getting our daily dose of beta carotene, vitamin C and a little extra vitamin A."

"How do you know that?" Iggy asked.

"Oh…" Snap's voice got a bit shaky. "My mom, she used to be a nutritionist and a total health nut. She taught us how to be healthy."

Iggy sensed some hesitation in Snap's voice. "Where is your mom anyway?" he asked.

Lizibeth poked Iggy in his side and gave him an odd look.

"She's not here," Snap replied.

The three stood there in an uncomfortable moment of silence. Iggy watched Lizibeth move her finger across her throat as if signaling to cut it out.

"What?" Iggy whispered back and shrugged.

"She's dead," Snap said.

"I told you not to ask." Liz crossed her arms. Snap Shell didn't come to school for two whole weeks after she died last year. And he never talked to anyone at school after that about his mom.

"It's alright," said Snap. "I've never really talked to any of my friends about it. It happened about a year ago. She got hit by a car."

The two lizards stood there speechless. After a long moment of silence, Iggy asked, "Are you still sad?"

"Not as sad as I used to be. Pops and I have been seeing a counselor. Talking about it totally helps, dude. I used to be really upset because the last thing I said to her was, *don't be late picking me up from school this time.* She was always late."

If Iggy knew one thing about turtles, it was that they were a bit slow. But he also knew Snap was being serious, so he kept his mouth shut.

"I wished I would have said something else like, *I love you.*"

Liz put her hand on Snap's shell and softly patted his back.

"I totally get it now. It was her time to go to heaven. She knew that I loved her and that my dad and I would be okay on our own. I think that's why he keeps the house really clean. My mom used to say, *a floor isn't clean until you can see your reflection in it.* He's keeping her memory alive."

"Where did your dad go?" Iggy asked.

"Probably in his study, working. Hey, you wanna see my room?" The turtle changed the subject.

"Totally!" Liz said and motioned to Iggy. Both lizards followed Snap to his bedroom.

"Wow! You really *do* like the beach…just like me!" Iggy shouted as they walked through the doorframe. Ocean waves were painted across each one of Snap's walls.

"I meant to tell you that your summer vacation story was totally sweet. I can't believe you actually got to surf and parasail," said Snap.

"It was my first time, but I bet you surfed all the

time in Galveston, huh?" Iggy asked, pointing to the surfboard mounted above Snap's bed.

"Not exactly." Snap laughed and held up his hand. "I can't swim, man."

"What? You're a turtle!" Iggy gasped.

"*Box shell* turtle," Snap responded.

"He doesn't have webbed feet." Liz giggled.

"Neither do we, but I can swim." Iggy smiled at Liz. "You've got a long tail! I am land only, dude."

Iggy held up his tail and said, "Well, that's the only thing this tail is actually good for."

All three animals cracked up at Iggy's joke. They didn't notice Mr. Shell walk into Snap's room while they were laughing. "Hello, kids."

Snap turned around at the sound of his dad's voice. "Oh hey Pops, these are my new friends from school, Iggy and Liz."

"Thanks for letting us come over, Mr. Shell." Iggy shook the turtle's hand.

"You kids are welcome back anytime," Mr. Shell said and smiled.

As the lizards headed home, they had a few minutes to chat before approaching Liz's house. "I would have never guessed that Snap's mom died," Iggy admitted. "Snap just seems so laid back."

"Seeing a counselor must have really helped because he used to not talk to anyone last year at school about his mom," said Liz.

"I wonder if Mr. Shell will get married again?" remarked Iggy.

"Maybe one day."

"I bet it's fun hanging out with his dad all day."

"Yeah, but I'm sure he misses not having a mom."

"Probably so," Iggy agreed.

The lizards stopped in Liz's front yard to say good-bye. "This is my house, so I guess I'll see you later," Liz said with a smile.

"Okay. See you at school." Iggy waved and continued his walk home. He had definitely learned a lot about his new friend.

Chapter Four

Brats Wear Pink

When Iggy walked into the kitchen for dinner, he noticed a cloud of smoke coming from the pot on the stove. "Uh, Mom…are these vegetables supposed to be smoked?"

"Oh, no!" Mrs. Green screamed as she darted to the stove. Iggy watched his mom open the pot and drop her head in disgust.

That night, dinner wasn't exactly perfect. The brussel sprouts were burnt, the broccoli was brown, and the asparagus was a bit tough.

"Peee-uuu!" screeched little Molly. "This broccoli smells like poo…."

"Don't be a brat!" Iggy interrupted his sister before

she could finish her sentence. "Everything isn't always going to be perfect, Molly. So what if mom burned dinner, at least we have a mom to make us dinner." Iggy crossed his arms and looked directly at his sister.

"Alright, alright, that's enough." Their mom stepped in. "I'm sorry I burned our food, but like Iggy said, everything can't be perfect all the time."

"I know Mom, and that's why Molly shouldn't be such a brat. Snap Shell doesn't even have a mom!" Iggy glared at his little sister and stuck his nose up in the air.

"Oh, your friend lost his mom?" asked his dad.

Molly sprang up from her chair, grabbed the green olive off her plate, and ran upstairs to her room in tears. Their mom followed her to calm her down.

"It's okay if this is bothering you, son." Mr. Green sat down next to Iggy. "We should talk about your friend and his mom. Molly will be fine once Mom talks to her."

Iggy asked a few questions and felt much better after talking to his dad. Later that night, Iggy sat on his bed thinking about the way he treated Molly. He knew he took his feelings out on his sister by yelling at her, so he decided to apologize. Iggy stood up and walked to Molly's bedroom. He slowly opened her door, but her room was empty. Suddenly, Iggy heard the sound of water running in the bathroom, so he tiptoed to the door and put his ear against it. He recognized the high-pitched humming of Molly's voice. After knocking and getting no response, he pushed the door slightly open, hoping Molly wasn't sitting on the toilet. When he peaked through the door crack, Iggy found his sister standing on top of the sink, wearing her pink robe and holding her baby doll upside down by the legs.

Molly looked up in surprise and screamed, "EXCUSE YOU! Can we please have some privacy? Can't you see that she's not dressed?" Molly quickly wrapped up her baby doll in a washcloth.

"Sorry about that. I just wanted to apologize for

snapping at you at the dinner table. I'll take you to the park tomorrow after school," he offered.

Molly was too focused on combing her doll's wet hair to hear what her brother had said. She probably had forgotten about the dinner incident anyway. Iggy shook his head and walked out of the bathroom. It must be nice to not have a care in the world like Molly. After a couple minutes of crying, she forgot why she was upset in the first place. However, he did feel better after apologizing. Snap reminded Iggy of a valuable lesson that day. Never go to bed mad at anyone in your family.

The next morning, Iggy hit the snooze button on his alarm clock and rolled back over in bed. As he lay there trying to get in a few more minutes of rest, he felt a thud right next to him. He opened his eyes to the sight of two big nose holes in his face.

"Molly? What in the world are you doing up?" Iggy groaned in a half-awake voice.

She quickly closed her eyes.

"You can't sleep in here, Molly," Iggy said.

Molly snarled in a creepy voice, "Just remember... the playground!" She jumped up and pranced back to her room.

"You're so weird," Iggy said and sighed and dragged himself out of bed. While he was brushing his teeth, he noticed his spikes were looking a bit flat. *Spike mousse will do the trick,* he thought and reached for the can. Iggy smoothed each of the spikes on the top of his head to a nice sharp point. "Much better!" he said out loud to the mirror. As he was finishing up, Mrs. Green passed by the bathroom on her way to Molly's room.

"Good morning, honey. Do you mind getting the table set for breakfast? I need to get your sister ready for school," Mrs. Green said and walked into Molly's room.

"Sure Mom," Iggy replied, as he walked out of the bathroom. He paused for a moment outside his sister's door. He noticed that Molly's baby doll was tucked beneath the covers of her bed, but no Molly.

He watched his mom put a pink dress on Molly's bed and walk over to the windowsill. She opened up the big pink chest where Molly kept all of her costumes. Sure enough, the little lizard was curled up and obviously pretending to be asleep, dressed in her pink Tinkerbell fairy costume.

"Molly, wake up! How many times have I told you not to close yourself up in this box?"

"Peter!" Molly screamed with relief. "You came! I knew you wouldn't let mean old Hook feed me to the alligators."

Iggy laughed under his breath.

"Yes, I have come to take you to school instead." Her mother played along. Molly's imagination was sometimes so big that there was no reasoning with her.

"No school!" Molly pouted.

"Either the alligators or school. You pick," her mom said with her hands on her hips. Molly climbed out of the storage chest and put on the pink dress that her mom had laid on the bed.

Iggy scurried down to the kitchen to set the table.

Molly's face lit up with excitement as she came downstairs. She sat down across from Iggy to a bowl of fresh berries. Her mother had picked the freshest strawberries, raspberries and blueberries from the farmer's market. "Yum!" she said just as the blueberries started to stain her upper lip. It looked as if she had been chewing on the wrong side of an ink pen.

"Nice mustache." Iggy shook his head and got up to pour a glass of orange juice. Molly's mother wiped her mouth with a wet dishrag before the blueberry stain set.

Molly squirmed and shooed her mother's hand away. "Gross!"

"Alright now, time to find your backpack. We don't want to be late picking up Little Bit," reminded her mother.

"You mean Olive?" Molly corrected her mom.

"Who's Olive?" Iggy asked.

"You know, my best friend."

"You would have an olive as a best friend."

"No, that's what I call her. She's my tiny turtle friend, but she looks like an olive…and I love olives! So, that's her new name."

"That's nice…well, got to go!" Iggy liked to walk to school and didn't have time to listen to such nonsense. Besides, he didn't want to miss Liz, who usually passed his house about now.

"Have a great day at school, honey."

"I will." Iggy snatched his backpack and darted out the door.

Chapter
Five

Mrs. Buff's Secret

At school, Iggy's teacher quickly walked to the front of the classroom and scribbled the morning instruction on the blackboard. "Now class," she said and cleared her throat then took a sip from the mug in her left paw. "I will be passing back your graded spelling tests while you write your personal narratives."

Iggy wasted no time. Writing had always been his favorite subject. Plus, he knew exactly what to write about. Changing schools proved to be his mom's best idea yet.

Iggy's concentration was interrupted when Mrs. Buff put something in the middle of the table. It was Kit Kat's test. Iggy curiously eyed Kit Kat to check out his reaction to his grade. Iggy figured a class clown like Kit Kat wouldn't do very well on a spelling test. Iggy took a quick peek and was stunned to see the number 100 and a smiley face at the top of Kit Kat's test. At that moment, Mrs. Buff stopped at Iggy's desk and handed him his spelling test with *98/A+* written on it.

A shiver passed through Iggy's body when he got a whiff of Mrs. Buff's breath. "Good job, Iggy," Mrs. Buff barked as she tiptoed away.

Kit Kat commented after seeing the grimaced look on Iggy's face. "Dog breath," he whispered. "You'll get used to it…all dogs have it *bad!*"

"Well, she *was* drinking coffee," Snap Shell butted in. "I heard that when you get old, you have to drink it just to stay awake."

"How do *you* know?" asked the black cat.

"Just do."

Liz giggled at Kit Kat when he rolled his eyes at Snap. Iggy quickly smirked at Liz.

"If you got a 100 on your test, please come up to

my desk to get a sticker," Mrs. Buff announced to the class.

"Hmmm, that would be me." Kit Kat stood up proudly, took in a deep breath of fresh air, and covered his nose as he walked up to the teacher's desk. All of the animals laughed as they watched the cat hand over his test.

When Mrs. Buff turned around to search through the cabinet for her special stickers, Kit Kat plopped down in her old wooden chair, trying to get another laugh from his captivated audience. "*Lady Jane Buff?*" he said to himself as he read the nameplate sitting on his teacher's desk. "What a name...and what a mess!" he said as he continued to snoop around. There was paper and junk everywhere. "Hmmm, what is this?" he said and pulled out a photo, which was hanging out of a closed drawer. "SICK!" Kit Kat dropped the picture and closely stared down at its contents. "What *are* those?"

"Well, Kit Kat..." Mrs. Buff sighed with her head still stuffed in a filing cabinet. Kit Kat quickly picked up the picture and put it behind his back when he stood back up.

"I will have to look for those stickers after lunch. I'm such a mess!"

"I'll say," Kit Kat whispered under his breath. "No problem. I have all that I need." The cat darted back to his seat before he got another whiff of Mrs. Buff's breath.

Iggy and his friends watched curiously as the cat took the time to brush away all the black hair in his chair before taking a seat. "What?" he smirked.

"You know what," Liz said. "What's in your paw?"

"Hey, I thought you got a hair cut last week, man," Snap added.

"You mean this?" Kit Kat quickly flashed the picture. "I don't know if I should let out Mrs. Buff's secret."

"Come on man, we won't tell," Snap waited for Kit Kat to spill his gossip.

"Okay, but it is probably the grossest thing I have ever seen. Mrs. Buff would be fired if Principal Horn knew that she was taking pictures of nasty creatures."

"What are they?" Snap Shell was losing his patience.

"I don't know. There are about five. They're hairless, brown, slimy, nasty little creatures. Oh, and they don't have faces. Sick."

"That seems pretty strange to me. Just show us," Snap said and sighed.

Kit Kat set the picture in the middle of his desk, and all three animals stood up and leaned over to look at the picture. "Ewww!" they all said together.

Iggy sat back in his seat and scratched his head. "Do you think they are part of a project for the science fair?"

"I'm not touching anything that looks like that," said the cat.

"I think our next chapter in science is about space. Maybe they are space aliens," Iggy said, trying to find a reason behind the mysterious picture.

"Please, there's no such thing," Liz said and rolled her eyes at Iggy.

"I'm serious!"

"Serious about what, Iggy?" Mrs. Buff had tiptoed over to determine what all the commotion was about. No one noticed that she had left her desk. "It's way too noisy over here."

Kit Kat snatched the picture and covered his mouth.

"Why is no one working on their writing assignment? Does someone want to tell me what's going on?" she asked while tapping her foot.

All four of the animals sat with their heads down in order to avoid making eye contact with Mrs. Buff.

"Well, if you four cannot come up with a reason for your behavior, then I will just take five minutes off of your recess time." Mrs. Buff walked back to her desk, and the group sat in silence. Everyone knew they could never admit that they had discovered her secret. Five minutes off recess was well worth keeping their mouths shut.

During recess, the four animals had to quietly sit on a bench with Mrs. Buff. As soon as their time was up, the animals ran out to meet their friends from Mr. Spike's fourth grade class on the playground. Naturally, Kit Kat brought out the picture, and the secret didn't stay a secret for long.

Chapter

Six

Don't Tell Liz

Kit Kat shouted across the playground, "Who wants to see a picture of space aliens?" Everyone ran over to the cat, who was waving the photo around in his paw. Iggy shook his head at the goofy cat because he knew that the picture would only get them all into trouble.

"Iggy thinks they are our class science project," Kit Kat told the kids who had crowded around him.

"I didn't mean that!" Iggy couldn't believe Kit Kat brought him into this.

All of a sudden, a large paw grabbed the picture. Kit Kat looked up to see Digger Dog, his worst enemy from last year, staring back at him. Digger was the biggest dog at school.

53

"How did you get a picture of my brothers and sisters?" Digger growled. Iggy knew that they were in big trouble.

"What! Those creatures are related to you?" Kit Kat meowed, noticing Digger's pointy teeth.

"You stole this from my Grandma Buff, didn't you?" Kit Kat had no idea that Digger was Mrs. Buff's grandson, but he did know when a dog wanted to fight him. He had been known to provoke a good number of dogs in his day. "You've definitely inherited your grandma's dog breath!" Kit Kat fanned his nose.

Before the big dog had a chance to react, Kit Kat darted up the nearest tree. His thick black fur stood straight up on his back. Digger ran after the cat, barking up at the tree. The crowd of animals followed to see what would happen next.

"You'll be sorry you ever messed with me. Watch your back, cat!" Digger howled.

Lizibeth noticed a sharp pain in the lower part of her tail. She turned and saw that Digger was jumping up and down on her tail, digging his nails into her. *"My Tail!"* she screamed.

"Get off her tail!" Iggy yelled at Digger.

The dog growled at Iggy and continued barking.

"That's enough!" A loud voice from the back honked. No one noticed that Principal Horn had come over to handle the trouble on the playground. Digger froze, and Liz pulled her tail to safety. *"Down, Digger! Down, Kit Kat!"* Principal Horn commanded.

Kit Kat slowly made his way down the tree, and the cat and dog were escorted to the principal's office. Recess was cut short, and Mrs. Buff's class was forced to sit inside with their heads on their desks in silence.

Just as Mrs. Buff turned the lights back on, an announcement came on over the loud speaker. "Iggy Green, please come down to the office."

"Ooooohhhhhh!" the whole class said in unison.

Iggy gulped.

"You're changing colors again, man." Snap pointed out. "Yikes." Snap bit his lip.

"Be brave Iggy. You didn't do anything wrong," Liz said trying to comfort her friend.

The walk to the principal's office was long and torturous. Iggy knew that either Kit Kat or Digger must have mentioned his name while explaining the situation regarding the picture.

Principal Horn greeted Iggy at the door and motioned for him to have a seat between the dog and the cat. "Now it is my understanding that you may be involved in this little escapade," Principal Horn said and cleared his throat. Iggy was afraid to look the big horn toad in the eyes. He was so intimidating.

Kit Kat whispered, "Sorry Iggy, I didn't mean to get you in trouble."

"Quiet, Kit Kat!" Principal Horn glared in Kit Kat's direction, bringing relief to the nervous lizard.

"I might have said something." Iggy decided to speak up.

"Like what? Puppies being a part of a science project? That sounds rather gruesome to me."

"I've never seen a newborn puppy before," Iggy said and sniffed as he looked down.

"Seriously. It was hard to tell what they were," Kit Kat added. Digger glared at the cat.

"You should have asked your teacher what they were, rather than stealing a picture of her grandchildren," said Principal Horn.

"My grandma had to miss her first day of school to take that picture," Digger added.

"Ohhh!" Iggy and Kit Kat looked at each other as it all started to make sense. Mrs. Buff was at the hospital the first day of school. Her daughter was having puppies. That was the emergency situation.

"Enough! Iggy, I trust that you are an honest lad, so I will let you off with a warning."

Iggy felt a sudden rush of relief to his pounding heart. He had never been in trouble before.

"As for the cat and dog fight on the playground, well, that is unacceptable at this school. You two will get notes sent home and will sit out during recess for a week." As the horned toad pulled out two discipline slips, he muffled in a lowered tone, "Iggy, scat before I change my mind."

The relieved lizard scurried to the door and back to class. Once he got to the classroom, his friends were already getting their backpacks ready to go home.

"So, did you get in trouble?" Liz asked.

"No, just a warning." Iggy smiled. "How's your tail?"

"It's okay. Mrs. Buff put a bandage on it." Liz held up her tail and continued, "I'm so glad you didn't get in trouble. I would have felt horrible, since I was kind of a part of it too."

"Kit Kat caused the whole thing. We better watch what we say around him next time," Iggy said. "I would have taken the blame for you any day though."

"You would?"

Iggy blushed and looked down at his feet.

Liz gave Iggy a quick hug. "See you tomorrow. My mom is picking me up." She darted to the door.

Snap and Iggy headed outside to walk home. As soon as they hit the pavement, the box shell spoke up, "It's so obvious, man."

"What's obvious?" Iggy asked.

"Someone has a girlfriend," Snap said grinning.

"What are you talking about? No I don't!"

"You and Liz," Snap said with a big grin on his face.

"I don't know what you're talking about."

"Please dude, you can't fool me."

"I'm not trying to. What are you getting at?" Iggy got a new knot in his stomach.

"I know you've got the hots for Liz!"

"What?! She's just my friend."

"Calm down, dude. Don't get your tail tied in a knot."

"I'm fine. I just don't want you to start anything," said the flustered iguana.

"Your secret's safe with me," Snap said and laughed.

Iggy could barely hold back a grin. He started to pick up his pace.

"Come on dude, slow down," Snap said.

"Sorry, guess it's just a habit."

"But you know that's how it all starts, dude."

"That's how what starts?" Iggy asked as he turned to walk up his driveway.

"Relationships!"

"Don't say that so loud." When Iggy got up to the door, he quickly turned around and yelled back at Snap, "Okay, just don't tell Liz!"

During the first part of dinner that night, not a word came out of Iggy's mouth. He had a lot on his mind and just couldn't get what Snap said out of his head.

Mr. Green blessed the food and prayed for speed and endurance for his big race on Sunday morning. Iggy realized that he had almost forgotten about his father's race after the hectic day he had at school.

"What kind of race are you running, Dad?" questioned Iggy.

"That's the first word you have spoken all night. Are you okay, Champ?"

"Yeah, it's just been a long day."

"I know how you feel. Today was my last day to train, so I did a long twenty-two mile run since Sunday is the marathon."

"A marathon is twenty-six miles, huh Dad?" Iggy asked and took a bite of salad.

"Pretty close, 26.2 to be exact," Mr. Green answered and scooped up some peas and put them on Molly's plate.

"I don't like peas, Daddy."

Iggy continued, "Didn't you come in fourth place at the Boston Marathon last year?"

"Sure did, and I have been training even harder this year."

"I can't wait till Sunday!" Iggy smiled at his father.

"Me too, Champ!"

That night, Iggy helped his mom do the dishes before heading up for bed. As he lay in bed, his mind kept replaying the crazy idea that Snap had so cleverly come up with. The words, *I know you've got the hots for Liz,* kept repeating over and over again in his brain. He had never felt so frazzled about anything in his life. Could it really be true? Could Iggy seriously have his first crush?

Buddy

Iggy left a little late for school the next morning, hoping to avoid being alone with Liz. It was hard for him to even look at her, let alone speak to her in class. There had been a huge knot in his stomach since last night.

"Iggy, what's wrong with you today?" asked Liz. "You're so quiet."

Iggy looked straight up at Snap who had a guilty grin on his face. "Nothing," Iggy replied defensively. "I, uh, I didn't get much sleep last night. Molly snores. Really loud, too."

"You can hear her all the way in your room?" Liz questioned.

Iggy couldn't come up with anything better on

the spot. He couldn't believe that he just made up a lie about his little sister. Luckily, Iggy didn't have a chance to explain any further because Mrs. Buff barked, "Can I have the class's attention, please? I would like to introduce a new student."

Everyone looked to see a brown bullfrog standing at the front of the class. "This is Buddy. He has just moved here from New York. Please make him feel welcome."

"They call me Bud back in the Bronx," the frog croaked as he hopped over to an empty desk.

Iggy exchanged a look with Snap. The turtle shrugged his shoulders at the iguana and started on his morning work.

At lunchtime, the class lined up to walk down to the cafeteria. Iggy noticed Bud hop straight up to the front of the line, as if he were the line leader or something.

Leave it to Kit Kat to open his mouth. "Hey, Buddy!" Kit Kat yelled from the back of the line. "Liz is the line leader today."

The bullfrog turned around and said, "Do I look like your buddy? It's Bud! Didn't you hear me earlier?" He turned his back to the cat.

"Nice back-warts," Kit Kat grunted under his breath.

"Stop it, Kit Kat," Liz pleaded. "It's not that big of a deal." Instantly, Iggy wondered if Liz wanted to stay in the back of the line next to him.

At lunch, Bud somehow managed to sit on the other side of Liz. Iggy sat down in his seat between Liz and Snap.

When Bud pulled out a smelly bag of dried flies from his lunch kit, Liz groaned, "Ewwww, you eat that?"

"Yeah," Bud said and flicked a fly on Liz.

"Yuck!" She shook off the fly, and it landed on her veggie burger.

"Jumpy lizard! Now look what you've done," the bullfrog croaked. "But if you aren't going to eat your burger now, I will."

Liz set the veggie burger in front of Bud. None of the other animals noticed what had happened.Liz sat with a frustrated look on her face.

"Man, Liz. You must have inhaled that burger. I'm only halfway done," Snap said, shocked.

"I gave it to Bud," she said sadly.

"Hey Liz, you know I get first dibs on your leftovers," said Kat Kat while chomping on his own lunch.

Iggy leaned in and looked over to see Bud stuffing the last of Liz's burger in his mouth. "Why did you give it to him? I thought you liked veggie burgers?"

"I love veggie burgers, but not topped with dried up flies," Liz sighed.

"Ha, who would?" Kit Kat laughed.

"Obviously him," Iggy said pointing at the hungry bullfrog who let out a loud burp.

Snap shook his head and glared at the bullfrog. Iggy cut his own burger in half and passed part of it to Liz. Bud showed no shame that he'd eaten Liz's lunch.

Snap changed the subject. "So Bud, why did you move to Texas, anyway?"

"That's none of your business," the frog grunted.

"You better watch your attitude, Bud, or it's going to be pretty hard to make friends around here." Kit

Kat jumped into the middle of the conversation.

"Like I care. If anyone messes with me, I'll just tell my grandtoad!"

"Okay, and what's he going to do about it?" Kit Kat challenged the frog.

"Ha!" Bud mocked the cat. "Don't you know Principal Horn?"

"WHAT?" Iggy jumped in. "The principal is your grandpa?"

"That's right, lizard. I live with him now. So don't mess with me." Bud hopped up from the table, leaving his trash behind.

"I just don't know about that frog." Snap put one finger up to his lip.

"Me neither," Kit Kat added. "What I would like to know is how can Bud be Principal Horn's grandson? Last time I checked, toads and frogs weren't in the same family. He's probably a liar, too!"

"I don't know about that. I think it's possible. I have iguanas, lizards and water dragons in my family," explained Iggy.

"Dude. Dragons?" Snap perked up.

"Yeah. My cousin, Dragon D, is my favorite dragon. He kind of reminds me of you, Snap."

"That's legit, man."

All the animals gathered their trash and got ready to head outside for recess.

Out on the field, the whole class played dodge ball. When it was Bud's turn to throw the ball, he continuously tried to get Liz out. One hard peg finally knocked Liz out of the game.

"Ouch! Why are you throwing so hard, Bud?" Liz ran to the side, far away from Bud. The rest of the group followed.

"I don't know what it is about that bullfrog, but he's starting to get on my nerves. I think he might have bruised my shell," said the box turtle as he slowly approached the group, who were already knocked out of the game. "What a bully!"

"I don't know what he could have against us. I mean, he's the new guy...at *our school!*" Iggy stomped his foot.

"I don't know either, but I'll figure it out," Snap said, seeming very determined.

The next morning as the group got ready for class to start, Liz let out a loud scream, "Ouch! That was my tail."

"Well then move it out of the walking path!" Bud croaked, hopping heavily to his seat.

"That frog hopped *hard* right on the tip of my tail! HOW RUDE!" Liz sighed.

Lunch was no better. When Iggy showed up at the lunch table with his tray in hand, Bud was sitting in *his* seat next to Liz. "We told him that was your seat Iggy," Kit Kat said to the stunned lizard.

"And I told them that these seats don't have anyone's names on them. Back in the Bronx, it's first come, first serve," Bud rudely replied.

Iggy didn't say anything and sat on the other side of Kit Kat.

On the walk home from school, Snap and Iggy had

a pretty serious conversation about the bullfrog from the Bronx. "You know what's going on, man?" Snap sounded like he had something to say. "You've got competition, dude."

"What kind of competition?"

Snap seemed to have great insight on a number of things the more Iggy got to know the wise box shell.

"That frog is trying to steal your girl," Snap informed the iguana.

"What? That's crazy! Bud is meaner to Liz than he is to Kit Kat!"

"Exactly! That's the problem. He doesn't know how to get a girl…no social skills."

"Soooo, what are you getting at?" Iggy still didn't get the point. "And Liz is not my girl."

"Hmmm. Haven't you heard? Some guys who don't know how to tell a lady they like 'em are just really mean and bully them instead."

"Well he does manage to find his way next to Liz everyday."

"Exactly. So he can pick on her. It's the same song

70

and dance man…pulling on her tail, pegging her with the ball, throwing flies on her food. I've seen this before."

"You have? So, what should I do about it?" Iggy asked the wise box shell.

"Confess your love to Liz, dude. Trust me, y'all are perfect for each other…long tails and all." Snap laughed and slapped Iggy on the back. "Ouch! Those scales are sharp!" Snap quickly pulled his hand inside his shell.

"Okay, that's enough. I think you're getting a little carried away. I can't say anything to Liz."

"So you admit it then. I knew it! You do like her."

"Oh, you think you're so clever. So what if I do, I could never admit it to Liz."

"How come? Are you scared?"

"HELLO! How long have we been friends? I can't exactly keep my cool in these kind of situations."

"Oh, you mean the whole color changing thing."

"Yeah, iguanas are supposed to stay green. I'm not a chameleon, you know."

"Hmmm, I could probably refer you to a good therapist. Have you ever heard of Anxiety Disorder?"

"I seriously don't have time for this. Plus, I don't have to worry about Liz and Bud. I bet she's afraid she'll get a wart if she gets too close to him."

"You're in denial, dude. I can't wait to tell you, *I told you so.*"

The Matchmaker

The following morning when Snap and Iggy walked into the classroom, Bud and Liz were at the pencil sharpener...TOGETHER! Iggy felt a wave of jealousy flood over him.

"DUDE, check that out!" Snap saw it too. "I told ya, man...he's sneaky. How's that denial now?"

"That's it. I need to sharpen *my* pencil, too!" Iggy stomped toward the sharpener. As he approached Liz and Bud, he heard the last of Bud's words.

"Just keep this between you and me," Bud whispered.

Iggy couldn't believe Bud had the nerve to make Liz keep a secret for him. What could he have possibly told her?

The bullfrog turned toward Iggy, looked him up and down, snorted, then hopped back to his seat.

"Yuck," Iggy said and shook his head.

"Hey, Iggy," Liz said, smiling.

"Are you done with the sharpener yet?" he asked.

"And good morning to you, too." The confused lizard walked away from the sharpener. "It's all yours."

Iggy realized that the tables had turned. Now *he* was being mean to Liz, and Bud was on her good side. He couldn't help but think this was all part of the bullfrog's plan.

During recess, Bud continually pulled Liz's tail and then hopped off as if he was flirting with her. That was the last straw. On Bud's third attempt to pull the lizard's tail, Iggy stood tall and yelled, "Get your hands off my Liz!"

"Your Liz? Did you hear that, Liz?" Bud asked, attempting to embarrass both lizards.

Iggy gulped. He meant to just say, *Liz*. He nervously looked at Snap. Snap along with the entire class stared at Iggy. Kit Kat rolled around on the ground

74

laughing in amusement. Iggy noticed that Liz had actually changed colors, matching his own shade of red. He had never seen her look so embarrassed.

Snap decided to speak up. "We all know you pull Liz's tail because you've got a huge crush on her! Face it man, BUSTED!"

Just then the whistle sounded bringing recess to an end, and everyone had to go back inside.

"Saved by the bell," Iggy said under his breath. He was dreading going back in the classroom. The anxious lizard could barely look at Liz as he walked back.

The class sat down at their desks to finish a reading assignment. Iggy could feel Liz turn her head toward him. He stopped reading. She whispered to Iggy, "Thanks for standing up for me, but you really should try to be nicer to Bud."

What? Nicer to Bud? Iggy could barely talk and stuttered, "You're welcome." He just wanted the day to end. Luckily, his dad was picking him up from school today for their traditional last run together before his dad's big race in the morning. Iggy was relieved that he wouldn't have to suffer through an awkward walk home with Liz, yet he was worried that Snap might spill his secret.

When the bell rang, Iggy said good-bye to his friends and went straight to the front of the school to wait for his dad. He watched Liz and Snap head down the sidewalk together. Iggy could only imagine what they were talking about.

Meanwhile, on the walk home, Snap wanted so badly to tell Liz that Iggy liked her, but he knew he couldn't break his promise to Iggy. He did manage to slip in a few questions, though. "So, do you like Bud or something?"

"No, Snap! What are you talking about?"

"Hey, you never know. I just thought I'd ask."

"Whatever. Bud's not exactly my type."

"Oh, so you have a type, eh?"

"What are you getting at Snap? Does Iggy think I like Bud?"

"Hey, who said anything about Iggy? But I'll make sure he knows you don't…if you want me to."

"Well, sure…if you want." Liz paused for a moment. "Okay, so can you keep a secret?" Liz asked.

Snap just *knew* that Liz was about to confess her love for Iggy, but instead she said, "We should really try to give Bud a chance."

"What! Why? I thought you liked Iggy," Snap accidentally blurted out.

Liz blushed. "This has nothing to do with Iggy."

"Then why should we be friends with that awful bullfrog?"

"Snap!" She stood there for a second with her hand on her hip and continued, "I'm not supposed to say anything, but Bud is having family problems."

Snap knew what it was like to have family problems after the death of his mom. "Okay. I'll try my best to give him a chance," Snap said as they arrived in front of Liz's driveway.

"Good. Iggy, too!" she said and smiled.

"Yeah, yeah," he said and sighed.

"Well, I'll see you tomorrow," Liz said as she turned to walk up to her house. Before she got to the door, she turned around and yelled to Snap, "Don't forget to tell Iggy that I don't...you know..."

"I know, I know. You're not in love with Bud," Snap said and laughed. "Oh, you won't have to worry. I'll remember," Snap whispered under his breath, grinning from ear to ear. "I knew it," he congratulated himself. "I'm such a matchmaker!"

The Marathon

Sunday morning, Iggy ran downstairs to show his dad the sign he had made for the race. To Iggy's surprise, Molly beat him to it. She was already eating breakfast in her pink cheerleading skirt with her own sign laying neatly on Iggy's chair. Iggy wondered why she looked so excited to be awake before the sun came up. It had to be because she actually had an excuse to wear that ridiculous pink costume.

"It's about time you came down, you lazy lizard!" Molly spoke with a British accent and threw a pom pom at her brother.

"Weirdo." Iggy rolled his eyes at Molly and took the sign out of his chair.

The whole family had to leave the house at five a.m. in order to get their father to the race on time. Iggy's dad liked to have time to mentally prepare and stretch before his 7 o'clock starting time.

Iggy and Molly grabbed their signs and headed out to the car. Naturally Molly's sign was covered in pink glitter and streamers. It said, *Run Daddy Run.* Iggy's sign was painted green and blue, and it read, *Go #45!*

At six a.m., Mr. Green started his hamstring stretches and jogged in place to warm up his muscles. Molly got on the ground and slid slowly into the splits, as if she were getting ready for a cheerleading competition.

"Molly, get out of the dirt before you ruin that skirt," her mom huffed.

"Mom, I mustn't pull a bone while I perform."

"You mean a muscle," Iggy corrected her.

"Whatever. I'm stuck. Someone get me up." Molly couldn't get up from her splits.

Iggy pulled Molly up off the ground. Finally it was time for Mr. Green to get in his starting position.

The family gave their dad one last good-luck hug and left him in the huge crowd, outside the Houston Convention Center. The team of three wanted to get a good spot right next to the second mile marker of the race, so they headed toward Capitol Street.

A booming voice echoed over the loud speaker. *Welcome to the Houston Marathon! Runners, you have five minutes until starting time.* Iggy always got nervous for his dad when he heard the time announcement.

"Oh, no!" Iggy screamed.

"What is it, son?" asked his mom.

"I forgot to tell Dad to *break a leg like* I always do!"

"It's okay. You wished him good luck, remember?"

"No, I always say it that way...it's special good luck," Iggy sighed.

"Pick me up! They are about to shoot the gun!" Molly jumped up and down, not empathizing with her brother.

"Fine. Come here then." Iggy tried not to worry as Molly started to crawl up his leg and onto his back.

"Why would you want Daddy to break a leg anyway, Iggy? That is RUDE."

"Hold on, you are pulling me down, Molly, and *break a leg* is just a saying."

"Then why does it matter?" Molly managed to make her way up to the top of her brother's back.

Iggy lifted her onto his shoulders. "OUCH! When was the last time you trimmed your toe nails?"

"Ewww! You're gross! Don't ask a lady such personal questions." Molly did a wobbly shoulder stand on Iggy's shoulders. Molly always made Iggy hold her sign as she stood on his shoulders, shaking her miniature pom poms.

"Molly, please sit on your behind so that you don't fall off of Iggy."

"Okay!" Molly wrapped her legs around her brother's neck for support.

"Ahhh...you're choking me," Iggy gagged.

"Here, take your poms, Molly." Mom handed the little lizard the tiny poms.

Molly went crazy, shaking and hooting in the air.

"Molly! Wait until they shoot the gun!"

"Oh yeah!" She started to giggle.

ON YOUR MARKS. GET SET. GO! The gun shot loud in the air, and Molly jumped with fright. "Eek! That dumb thing scares me every time."

Ten minutes into the start of the race, number forty-five was right on his race time.

"Here comes your father, children…right on time." Mr. Green was one of the first to come around the corner.

"Man! That was fast, huh, Mom?" Iggy asked.

The family screamed and held up their signs as Mr. Green sped by them. He gave them a quick wave and continued his race.

"Now what mile, Mama?" asked little Molly.

"Well, your dad usually likes to eat his protein bar around mile eight, so we will meet him by Memorial Park. He should be there in about thirty minutes," she informed the kids.

Iggy had his dad's first protein bar ready to go, but when thirty minutes came around, Mr. Green was nowhere to be found.

"Did we miss him, Mom?"

"Give him a few more minutes," Mrs. Green encouraged her son.

Five minutes passed, and at least fifteen runners had sped by…mostly lizards.

"Mom, does this mean that Dad is not going to

win?" Iggy asked. He realized that his mom never answered his question and seemed a bit on edge. Ten minutes later, there was still no sign of Mr. Green.

"This is so strange," Mrs. Green said under her breath. "He's never averaged more than an eight-minute mile, not even on a bad day."

Iggy heard the shrill of an ambulance's siren in the distance.

"Follow me, kids!" Mrs. Green headed to the first aid station back at the seventh mile marker.

"Where's Daddy? Why are we going back?" Molly asked.

Iggy picked up his little sister and quickly followed his mom. When the family reached the seventh mile, they saw a lizard on a stretcher.

"Is that Dad?" Iggy squealed.

"Don't move from this spot. I don't want to lose you in the crowd," Mrs. Green said. She told Iggy to stay with his sister right next to a big, blue port-a-potty.

Molly covered her eyes with her pom poms and started crying. The crowds of animals were scaring her. Iggy wanted to calm his sister down, but he was too worried.

"Can't we hide in this blue house, Iggy?" Molly asked as she reached for the door handle to the portable toilet.

"No, Molly, that is not a house." The last thing Iggy needed was to deal with Molly's reaction once she realized what was inside the blue *house*.

"It's all my fault," he told himself. "I bet Dad broke his leg because of me."

After what seemed like an hour, Mrs. Green came back to the port-a-potty.

"Is he okay, Mom? How bad is Dad?"

"That wasn't your father, children. I just asked one of the race supervisors, and he said forty-five is winning the race! Your father should be around mile sixteen by now!"

"WHAT!" Iggy screamed.

"That's right, kids. If we hop in the car and head toward Montrose Boulevard, we should be able to meet him at the twentieth mile marker."

"I can't believe it! I thought Dad broke a leg." Iggy sighed in relief. "What are we waiting for? Let's go!" Iggy started to jog for the car.

"Wait! Wait for me," Molly yelled. Iggy grabbed Molly and put her on his back. Molly wiped her tears and managed to put a smile back on her face. "Piggy back ride," the little lizard chirped.

When the family got to mile twenty, they hoped that they hadn't already missed him.

"I don't know how we missed your father. I thought we timed it perfectly."

Iggy was just happy that his dad hadn't broken anything. Iggy barely had time to pick up his sign when one single lizard, running like lightning, came around the corner.

"Look, it's Dad!" Iggy scrambled to get out the protein bar. Mr. Green spotted his family... thanks to Molly and her hot pink poms. He slowed down to a steady jog and met his family by the curb.

"Where have you been?" Mr. Green was breathing heavily, but continued to jog as he talked.

"Dad, we were afraid you got injured," Iggy said while jogging on the grass along side of his father.

"Me? Never." Mr. Green laughed at his son, peeling open the protein bar that Iggy gave him.

"We didn't see you, Daddy, so we thought Iggy cursed you and broke your leg." Molly tried to explain as she yelled from behind, but it became even more confusing.

Mr. Green laughed and shook his head. "I would love to chat, but I've got to put this new energy to good use and finish this race. I'm winning, you know."

"We know, Dad, you're in first place. Only six more miles to go," Iggy shouted to his dad as he jogged backwards and waved bye to his family. Mr. Green got smaller and smaller as he picked up his pace back to less than a five-minute mile.

"Let's go to our next stop kids and meet your father."

Molly jumped in and screamed, "AT THE FINISH LINE!" Molly started to do her little dance number and shook her tail from side to side, wiggling her hips in unison with her poms.

By the time the family got down to the finish line, there were already thousands of animals gathering around, but the Greens wanted to get a close spot so they could see Dad win.

"What will Dad win, Mama?" asked little Molly.

"Well, if he wins first place, $50,000!"

"WHAT?" Iggy's eyeballs almost popped out of their sockets.

"Yeah, this is the race your dad has been training for all year."

"I hope Dad wins. What would we do with all that money?" Iggy looked at his mom.

"We could go to Disney World in Florida to see Tinkerbell!"

"Do you really think Dad would want to see a *fairy* over going to a beach, Molly?" Iggy sarcastically asked. "Think about it."

The lizards' argument about vacations got cut short when Mrs. Green cried out, "Here come two lizards… neck and neck!"

"Oh no, what does second place get?" asked Molly.

"Hold up your poms and cheer, Molly!" Iggy encouraged.

"Alright, alright." Molly hopped on top of her brother's back, digging her unclipped toe nails into his scaly skin.

"AHHHH! That hurts!"

Mr. Green was still right in line with the other lizard. It looked like there was going to be a tie.

"Will they have a tie breaker?" As Iggy kept a close eye on his dad, he noticed that it looked as if his father wasn't moving. His arms and legs were moving back and forth, but neither runner was getting much closer to the finish line.

"What is taking them so long?" Molly huffed. "I thought Daddy could run faster than that."

"I guess he finally *hit the wall*," said Mrs. Green.

"What? I don't see a wall!" both lizards said at the same time.

"Oh no, not a real wall," their mother laughed. "*Hitting the wall* is a saying that runners use when their bodies are so tired their muscles almost stop working."

"Oh. Poor Daddy." Molly frowned.

The runners were now only twenty yards away from the finish line. The cameras were ready to snap a photo finish in case proof was needed to decide the winner. The clock read two hours, twelve minutes, and eight seconds when dad finally made it over the finish line with the other lizard by his side. He fell to the ground as soon as he crossed and the crowd cheered.

"Who won?" Iggy asked.

"We don't know yet, we have to wait for the snap shot to know the final results," Mom explained.

"AND THE WINNER IS," the loud speaker announced. "NUMBER FORTY-FIVE, IGWARD GREEN...BY A LONG TOE!"

"A toe?" Molly made a funny looking face and scrunched her nose. "Eww, gross!"

Igward Green had definitely won because his middle toe had crossed over the finish line before anything else.

Tomatoes

By Monday morning, Iggy was crawling with excitement to get to school. He couldn't wait to tell his friends all about his dad's race, especially Liz. The weekend had helped Iggy forget his anxiety about the playground incident with Liz and Bud last Friday.

"It was so intense! Two runners, side by side. It looked like someone had hit a *s-l-o-w m-o-t-i-o-n* button, and then my dad collapsed to the ground as if every muscle in his body turned to jelly," Iggy explained.

"What do you think your dad will do with all of that money?" Snap inquired.

"Uh, put it in our college fund, I suppose," Iggy replied.

"I would buy a surfboard for sure!"

"Snap, you're not a water turtle," Liz teased and cocked her head toward her shoulder.

"Dude. Don't shatter my dream," Snap said.

"I just can't believe he won. Are you going to start racing like your dad?" Liz asked.

"I've thought about it, but baseball is really my thing."

"You play baseball?" Liz asked.

"Yeah, I'm on a little league team, but I'm looking for a new one this year."

"You should try out for the STARS!" Snap and Liz both said at the same time.

"Wait, you both play?"

"Well, I play softball, but my dad coaches the STARS," Liz said.

"Catcher," Snap said nodding. "How about you?"

"Pitcher," Iggy said. He was MVP last year on his little league team.

"Awesome! So, when can we meet your dad?" Liz asked.

"I have an idea. Both of you should come over to my house for dinner."

"Great idea," said Liz smiling.

Iggy blushed and tried not to make eye contact with Snap, who was snorting under his breath.

"I want to meet your little sister too," Liz said.

Iggy figured Liz would probably love little Molly.

"Okay, how about you both come over tomorrow. I'm sure my parents won't mind. Maybe we could play catch in the backyard too." This would be Iggy's chance to show off his baseball skills in front of Liz and get her to forget all about Bud.

The next day, Iggy reminded Snap and Liz that dinner would be at six o'clock. "We're having veggie lasagna, asparagus and fruit salad," Iggy announced.

"Those are three of my favorite things," Liz squeaked.

"Okay, I'll see you guys at six," Snap said to the lizards as he turned around to go meet his father at the front of the school. "Pops and I are going down to Buffalo Bayou to hang out with a few of his old turtle buddies."

"Later, Snap!"

Iggy started to get an uncomfortable feeling in his stomach when he realized he would be walking home with Liz by himself today. He tried to think of something interesting to talk about, but Liz had lots to say, which took the pressure off of him.

"Turtles," she sighed. "They're always hanging out at bayous. I just don't get it."

Iggy nodded his head to agree, even though he never realized it was something turtles do.

"Frogs too…they like hanging out at the bayou more than turtles. Speaking of frogs…"

Here we go. Iggy wasn't expecting the conversation to turn to bullfrogs.

"So, I was talking to Snap about Bud the other day."

"Oh, really?" Iggy asked with hesitation. Snap

never had a chance to fill Iggy in on his conversation with Liz.

"I don't like him, you know, but I am trying to be his friend. I mean you know what it's like to be the new guy."

Iggy didn't respond to Liz, because all he could think about was, what if Liz had only made friends with him because he was the new guy too?

"Iggy, did you hear me?" Liz waved her hand in front of his face.

"Oh, sorry. Uh, I know what you mean."

"And actually, I'm not supposed to say anything, but Bud is having family problems." Before Liz could explain any further, they were already in front of Iggy's house. He wondered if he should walk Liz all the way to her house this time. Snap usually walked the rest of the way with her. He thought he should offer, but the words didn't seem to come out right.

"Do you want me to home you walk? I mean walk you home?" Iggy could feel heat rush to his cheeks.

"It's okay. I can see my mom in our front yard from

here. Thanks though. We can finish talking about this some other time. See you tonight." Liz kept walking, and Iggy headed up his driveway.

As it got closer to six, Iggy helped his mom set the table for dinner. He paced around the kitchen looking for plates.

"Iggy, what are you looking for? You are acting like you have never set a table before," his mom said laughing.

"Um, just plates. Look, I found them!"

"You've been overly excited lately. What's going on?"

"It's nothing Mom."

Iggy's mom had no idea how hard it was to be a nine-year-old with a crush. Just then, Iggy heard the doorbell ringing.

"Oh no, they're here!" Iggy moaned.

"It's okay son, calm down."

Moments later, Iggy turned around to find Molly hand in hand with Lizibeth.

"Your girlfriend is here, Iggy. She's pretty." Molly must have been spying out the window; she had been so quick to answer the door. Molly giggled and ran back upstairs.

With a shaky voice, Iggy awkwardly introduced his mom to Liz.

"Nice to meet you Liz. Iggy has told me so much about you."

"Mom!" Iggy didn't want Liz to think that he talked about her to his mother.

Ding Dong. Saved by the bell, again.

"I'll get it!" Iggy raced away.

"Hey man. Where's your dad?" Snap eagerly asked as Iggy opened the door.

"You'll meet him in a second. He's hanging out in the living room. Let's go get Liz."

When Snap and Liz turned around toward the living room, they did not expect to see what they saw. Iggy literally meant *hanging*! Mr. Green was hanging upside down by his tail from some kind of device coming out of the ceiling.

"Dad, they're here!" Iggy spoke as if there was nothing strange about hanging from the ceiling.

"Hi you two. Give me a second, and I'll climb on down." Snap and Liz stared with curiosity to see how Mr. Green would manage to get back on his feet. As the muscular lizard pulled himself up in a sitting position, his tail came loose, and he hopped down onto both feet.

"Sweet," said Snap.

"Just stretching out my spine. I have to do that after every long race," Mr. Green explained.

"Oh, of course. Congrats on your win." Snap stuck out his hand for a fist bump.

"Thank you, son. You must be Snap Shell."

"And this is Liz." Iggy motioned his hand at the lizard.

Mrs. Green announced that dinner was ready, so everyone headed to the dining room. Iggy was impressed by his mom's presentation of dinner. They were actually using the matching plates and forks, normally saved for special occasions. *Nice touch,* he thought to himself. The lasagna smelled delicious. His mom totally pulled through and thankfully hadn't burned anything this time. Iggy smiled when he noticed that his mom had put his lime green glass next to Liz's pastel pink one.

Mrs. Green yelled upstairs, "Molly! Dinner's ready!"

"Coming, madam," Molly sang from the top of the stairs.

Everyone turned around to see Molly, in a pink tutu, leap from the top stair to the floor and land on one foot while squealing, "LAAAA!" Once she landed and held her position, she wobbled and fell to the floor.

"That was a somewhat graceful landing," her mom said.

"RATS!" she groaned, picking herself up off of the floor. "Let me do it once more."

"No ma'am. It's time for dinner. Remember, we have company," Mom said.

"But a ballerina always lands her leaps." Molly raced back up the stairs.

"Molly!"

"Okay, okay. I'm coming." She turned around and

skipped into the dining room and performed one last arabesque on one foot and a pointed toe.

"Showoff," Iggy mumbled under his breath.

"You will have to forgive our little ballerina here," their mom said. "She just came from ballet class. That means she'll be leaping around the house for the rest of the night."

Lizibeth giggled and told the little lizard, "I love your pink tutu."

"Thanks, so do I." Little Molly stood with a cute smirk on her face.

"Obviously. You wear it everyday," added her big brother.

"Molly, sit down so we can bless the food," Mrs. Green said and patted the chair next to her.

After the prayer, everyone started to dig in.

"Iggy, will you pass me the salad, please?" Liz asked.

"Sure." When Iggy reached over to pick up the bowl, he accidentally knocked over Molly's glass of grape juice into her bowl of asparagus.

"Leaping lizards! Watch it!" Molly screamed.

"Ah man. Sorry, Molly."

"It's fine by me. Now I don't have to eat those slimy asparagus spears. I've never been a fan of this particular vegetable," Molly said as she reached for a serving of green olives. Molly looked down at Iggy's shaky hand as he tried to wipe up the mess he made. "So, young sir," Molly grinned and continued as she unfolded her napkin to blot her upper lip. "Please do tell how you and your girlfriend met."

Everyone looked around the table, surprised by the young lizard's question.

Just then, Mr. Green said to Molly, "Molly Sue, leave your brother alone." He couldn't help but crack a grin at his daughter's guilty smile.

Snap Shell couldn't hold it in any longer. He busted out laughing, and a cherry tomato flew straight out of his mouth and smacked Iggy in the middle of his forehead.

"Oh, no! I'm sorry, dude," Snap said coughing. "Your sister's hilarious."

At that moment, everyone at the table started

laughing. Everyone but Iggy. It was bad enough that this dinner with Lizibeth was making him sweat, but now everyone was laughing at him.

Play Ball

"Okay, it was an accident," Mrs. Green spoke up.

"Sorry, Iggy, I couldn't help it," Snap admitted.

"It's cool," Iggy said and shrugged, pretending not to care.

Lizibeth quickly changed the subject. "So, Mr. Green, what was the hardest part about running the marathon?"

Iggy's thoughts had completely left the dinner table, and he never heard the answer to Lizibeth's question. His mind wouldn't stop racing. What could he do to not look like such a loser to Liz? He had to redeem himself. Maybe he could show off his batting skills in the backyard.

"Iggy...son...are you listening?" Mr. Green was now asking from across the table.

"Yes, we should play ball in the backyard," Iggy suddenly spoke up.

"What?" Molly shook her head at her big brother.

"Son, I think you got off topic. We're not talking about baseball, but I was asking you a question." Mr. Green had a concerned look on his face.

"Iggy what has gotten into you?" his mom asked.

"Yes, where are your manners? Daydreaming at the dinner table."

"Sorry, Dad. What were you asking me?"

"Nevermind about that. Baseball, huh? You guys should play after dinner," said Mr. Green.

"Well, if Liz wants to." Iggy turned to Liz.

"Sounds good to me!"

Iggy took his last bite of dinner. "I guess we should get started before it gets dark." Iggy stood up and walked to the back door.

Molly turned to Snap and said, "You want to give me a ride?"

"You want to ride on my back?" he questioned.

"Yes, on your shell, please. I mustn't mess up my freshly painted toe nails in the grass."

Snap looked down at Molly's feet. They were bright pink. Molly must have taken Iggy's advice and manicured her toes.

"Sure, hop on," Snap said.

Molly hopped on Snap's shell. "Come on you two lovebirds," she said over her shoulder.

Iggy should have known that Molly would tag along and continually try to embarrass him. He turned around to Liz. "Sorry about my little sister, she can be a real pain sometimes."

"Don't be so worried. If she knows it bothers you, she will do it even more."

"Yeah, I'm starting to pick up on that," Iggy agreed and decided to ignore Molly's teasing remarks. Both lizards walked out the back door. Molly started singing the wedding march as Iggy and Liz came throught the door together.

"Hey Molly, if you hand me the ball, I will throw it

to you," Iggy said hoping to distract Molly.

"Oh, okay." Molly didn't have anything else to say. She handed him the ball. "Here you go."

"Now stand back, and I will pitch it to you."

Molly picked up the bat, which was almost bigger than her. Iggy threw the ball, but Molly could barely swing the bat.

"This thing is too heavy. I quit!" Molly darted to the door, blew a kiss and said, "I have more important work to do." She shut the door.

"Okay, now we can really play!" Iggy cheered.

Snap picked up a ball, and Iggy picked up a bat.

"You can be our cheerleader," Iggy told Liz.

"What makes you think I can't play just as good as you guys?" Liz challenged.

"Oh, well I just figured."

"You figured softball isn't as hard as baseball? Give me that bat!" she demanded.

Iggy graciously handed Liz the bat.

"Show me what you got Snap!" Liz shouted.

"Why don't we have Iggy throw? He's a real

pitcher." Snap tossed the ball to his buddy.

Iggy caught the ball and looked across the yard at Liz, who had now turned from a bright shade of lime green to a sandy tan color, resembling the brown tree trunk behind her. He could barely make out the difference between her body and the tree. Iggy pitched it softly to her, but Liz just stood there with her hand on her hip.

"That was weak!" she mocked. "Don't you have a curve ball or fast ball up your sleeve?"

"Alright...I hope you can handle it." Iggy picked up the ball and threw it with lightning speed, certain Liz wouldn't see it coming. To his surprise, Liz hit it clear across the yard and over the neighbor's fence.

"Wow!" the boys said staring in amazement.

"Now that's what I'm talking about," Iggy said. Iggy was definitely impressed by Liz's batting skills. He even thought she could probably teach him a thing or two to help improve his own swing.

"You should join our summer league," Snap said and nudged Iggy in the side.

"Already on one boys," she said with a smile.

"How did you learn to swing like that?" Iggy asked.

"From my dad, he used to coach the Rough Riders baseball team."

"Wow. For real?" Iggy asked. Liz mentioned that her dad coached, but not for a minor league team.

As Liz turned around to get a new ball, Snap gave Iggy a quick wink. "I told you so…"

"Shhh, keep cool Snap."

After a few more rounds of ball, Snap noticed the street lights come on from across the way. "Well, it's time for me to head home, you two. Pops said he would pick me up when the street lights come on." Snap handed Iggy the catcher's mitt.

"Maybe we should go in too. I think a mosquito just bit my tail. Plus my mom should be on her way," Liz said as she handed the bat to Iggy.

After saying good-bye to Snap, the lizards headed upstairs to the game room. Iggy wanted to find a way to show Liz his baseball trophies. He wanted her to know he was a star on his little league team.

The opportunity to show off passed quickly when he looked out the window and saw a car pull into the driveway.

"My mom's here. Better go," Liz said.

Iggy would have to wait till next time...if there would be a next time. No telling what Bud might pull next week.

As they turned around to head downstairs, Iggy's tail managed to find its way in front of Liz's right foot. Liz pivoted and stepped down on the long, spiky thing, letting out a loud, "Ahhh! *Spikes!* Those things are sharp!"

"I'm so sorry! Is your foot okay?" Iggy was going to have to start putting a caution sign on his tail.

"Yeah, it just surprised me. I'm good though."

Iggy stayed behind Liz, shaking his head as they walked to the front door. "Are you sure you're okay?"

"Yes, I'm fine now. Next time we should play more ball."

"It's a deal, but you may want to wear shoes for your own protection," he joked.

Liz giggled as she hugged Iggy good-bye. He watched her walk to her mom's car. Just as Iggy was about to shut the door, she stopped and turned around to say one more thing, "By the way, that's some arm you've got."

The smile that grew on Iggy's face made his cheeks hurt. "Thanks. See you later." Iggy's plan may have just worked.

Dragon D

Over the next couple of weeks, Iggy constantly found himself trying to outdo Bud in everything. Sports, school, gym class, time alone with Liz…but nothing seemed to help Iggy stand out. Snap tried to reassure him that Liz didn't like Bud, but they both found it rather strange how much time she and the frog spent together. They always seemed to be talking about something at recess. Even though Iggy tried his hardest to be nice to Bud because of Liz, he still had the suspicion that Bud was trying to win her over just to get under Iggy's scales. He needed a new plan.

Luckily, Iggy's older and much more mature cousin, Dragon D, would be coming to stay for the weekend. Iggy knew he could ask his cousin for some advice.

Dragon D was the coolest, not to mention the fastest runner Iggy had ever seen. Even faster than his father.

Dragon D was the son of Mr. Green's brother. On Iggy's dad's side of the family there were many relatives who came from a particular breed of lizard called the water dragon. Iggy felt pretty lucky to have dragons in his family.

Iggy couldn't wait to hang out with his cousin on Friday night. His parents were going out on a date, so Dragon D would probably take Iggy and Molly out in his new convertible. When class was dismissed on Friday, he ran home because he knew Dragon D would be waiting at the house.

Sure enough, when Iggy opened the door, Dragon D and Molly were wrestling on the ground. Dragon D pulled Molly off the floor and ran over to greet his cousin. "Iggy! What's happening, little cuz?" Cousin

D held out his hand for a low five. "You two want to go get a smoothie or something?" Dragon D asked.

"Before dinner?" Molly questioned with her hands on her hips.

"No... *for* dinner!" Cousin D mocked back with his hand on his hip. "What, do you not like strawberry banana smoothies?"

"No. I love them. Let's go!" Molly said excitedly.

"Hey Cousin D, can I ask my two best friends to come?"

"You mean your girlfriend, Liz?" Molly asked with a giggle.

"Girlfriend? How old are you about to be?" Dragon D asked.

"Ten, this February." Iggy paused and said, "But she's not my girlfriend, and never mind. Maybe it should just be the three of us anyway." Iggy rolled his eyes.

"No man. I want to meet this Liz."

"Molly you have a big mouth for such a tiny head," Iggy snapped back at his little sister.

"Hey. I resent that! And if Iggy gets to take his friends, I'm bringing Olive."

"You want to bring an olive?" Dragon D questioned.

"No my best friend, Olive."

"You mean Little Bit? Forget it. Let's just go." Iggy knew that bringing up his friends in front of Molly had been a bad idea.

"Alright, alright. We'll talk when Molly goes to bed. I'm sure I'll meet her at your birthday party." Dragon D followed Iggy to the door.

"Wait! Don't leave me!" Molly screamed and ran to catch up.

The three lizards walked out the door and down the driveway to Dragon D's bright green Mustang convertible.

"I get the front seat." Molly sprinted to the car.

"Not so fast, little one, you aren't big enough to sit in the front yet," Dragon D reminded the little lizard.

"Yeah, you need a car seat," Iggy said and laughed.

"Whatever. That was like two years ago." Molly

climbed over the side of the car and landed on her face in the back seat.

"Nice. That was graceful." Iggy and his cousin laughed. When they turned around to look at Molly, she was sitting back with her shades on, legs up and arms resting on the back of the seat above her head.

"Wow. Little Miss Hollywood," Dragon D said laughing at Molly's dramatic mannerisms.

"Just drive gentlemen," Molly said, playing it cool.

"Where does she learn these things?" Dragon D looked over at Iggy. "Because we know she didn't get it from you."

"When I'm old enough to drive, I'm getting a Mustang convertible, just like this one, but it will be hot pink," Molly said from the backseat.

"Molly, first of all, they don't make pink cars, and besides, by the time you're old enough to drive, this car will be out of style." Iggy turned around and pulled on Molly's tail.

"Mustangs don't go out of style, bro." Dragon D

defended his prized possession.

"See. And my car will fly by then, too. You're just jealous."

"Yeah, yeah." Iggy shook his head.

Dragon D put the car in gear and zoomed off toward the smoothie shop.

"Leaping lizards, it's cold back here!" Molly zipped up her coat and pulled her hood over her head.

Dragon D found a parking spot and put up the car's convertible top. "We may want to keep the top up on the way back," he said, realizing that it was a bad idea to drop the top in January.

"I'll say. That wind froze my nose." Molly tried to sniff.

Dragon D ordered three strawberry banana smoothies, and they all sat down on a bench outside the smoothie shop.

"Maybe we should have gotten hot cocoa," Iggy said, rubbing his hands together.

"Too bad it isn't March yet," said Dragon D.

"I wish. I'm just ready for baseball," Iggy said.

"I like summer best because I don't have to go to school," Molly said as she tried to suck a fresh strawberry up her straw. "Mine's clogged!" the little lizard cried while shaking her cup up and down.

"Patience little one. If you blow through your straw, I bet you can shoot that berry straight across the street," Dragon D suggested.

Molly took the straw and blew as hard as she could. She blew so hard that the strawberry rocketed straight across the parking lot and landed on the front windshield of a white car that had just backed into a parking spot.

"Score!" she screamed.

"Oh, no!" Dragon D ducked with embarrassment as two lizards opened their doors to get out of the car.

"That was awesome!" Molly cheered.

"I bet that lady lizard and her daughter don't think…" Iggy's words froze. "Oh no," Iggy groaned.

"What? Do you know them? Is she your principal?" Dragon D kept asking questions.

"No," Molly squeaked. "Even better, that lovely

lizard is the one and only Lizibeth…Iggy's little girlfriend." Molly started clapping her hands together.

"And you just pegged them with a strawberry bullet," Iggy reminded her.

Lizibeth's mom stood by her car, looking at the berry burst. Lizibeth looked over to see where it came from. Molly waved back and forth at the two of them.

"Seriously Molly. Do you have to act like a monkey?" Iggy could only guess what kind of impression he had made on Liz's mom.

As the two lady lizards started walking toward the smoothie shop with disgusted looks on their faces, Iggy began to turn his usual shade of bright red.

"Relax Iggy, it was Molly's fault." Dragon D tried to calm Iggy down.

"Iggy? Is that you?" Liz yelled as she squinted toward the sun that was affecting her view.

"Hey Liz. Yep, it's me." Iggy stood up to wave.

"And me!" Molly stood up on her chair.

Liz had a questioning expression on her face. "So, did you?"

"No! That was Molly." Iggy jumped to his own defense.

"Sorry about that … my straw was plugged," Molly said giggling, admitting to hitting their car with the berry.

Liz introduced her mom to Iggy and Molly, and Iggy introduced his cousin to Liz and her mom.

"My mom is taking me to the doctor, so we've got to hurry," Liz informed the group.

"Are you sick?" asked little Molly.

"No, but I do have to get a flu shot." She cringed when she said the word, shot.

"We're getting smoothies before we go. It always calms Liz down," her mom said to little Molly. "Nice to meet everyone." As the lizards walked inside, Liz's mom turned around to add, "I would lay off the cherry bombs."

"It was a strawberry," Molly squeaked.

Iggy pulled his sister down by her tail. "Can we go now?" Iggy had enough. They headed back to the car. Dragon D took Molly's hand and helped her into the car this time.

Back at the house, Iggy turned on a basketball game while Dragon D put Molly to bed.

"Who's playing?" Dragon D pointed to the game on TV when he got downstairs.

"Rockets and the Mavs."

"Sweet! This should be good."

"Yeah, I just can't wait for baseball season."

"I hear ya."

Iggy and Dragon D were huge Chicago Cubs fans. Iggy's favorite memory was the time his dad took him and his cousin all the way to Chicago to watch a game at Wrigley Field. Iggy would do anything to go back.

"Didn't your dad say he was getting season tickets to the Astros this year?" Dragon D asked his little cousin.

"Yep, he's already got 'em." Iggy grinned.

"That'll be sweet. I wonder if he needs anyone to go in his place with you for a game or two?" Dragon D hinted.

"Maybe we could get you season tickets too. It would be just like the three of us in Chicago."

"That would be cool," Dragon D said then paused for a moment. "So. What's up with Liz? She seems cool." He wasted no time getting to the good stuff.

"You should see her swing a bat. She knocked it clear over the fence!"

"That little thing?" Dragon D questioned Liz's strength, considering her size.

"Yeah, her dad coached the Rough Riders."

"Really? I bet Uncle Igward and her dad would really get along," Dragon D said, lifting his brow.

"That's not the half of it. She's smart, funny, outgoing, but..." Iggy paused and said, "She's not my girlfriend."

"What! Why not? I had my first girlfriend in the fourth grade."

"You did? Who?"

"Darleen Dragon. She could run like the wind." Dragon D spoke as if he were still in love. "So what's your deal, and why is she not your girlfriend?"

"Well, there's this other guy."

"There always is." D shook his head slowly. "But

you shouldn't let that stop you. Who is this guy, anyway?"

"Bud the Bullfrog."

"What, he's a frog? Man, you've *so* got this one. Unless she's hoping he turns into a prince," he joked.

"I don't know. This guy is sneaky. Every day this week he tried to get ahead of me in the lunch line so he could sit next to Liz; plus he's always telling her secrets."

"Hmmm," D said and scratched his head. "It sounds like this frog knows you're interested. You better make a move and quick."

"A move? Like what? I'm not a fighter, D."

"Not a punch, dude…a move. You know, let her know what's up."

"Okay, so what kind of *move* do you suggest, D?"

"Alright…listen closely." Dragon D took a moment to get situated and comfortable in his chair. "All girls like flowers, so I picked a flower for Darleen out of my mom's flowerbed. I gave it to her on the playground…in front of everyone."

"Everyone? I don't know if I could do that, but I could pick a flower and maybe give it to her behind a tree or something more private."

"Do it man," Cousin D encouraged Iggy.

"Okay, I will. Mom's daisies are still alive."

"See, that's a sign that you should do it."

The Last Daisy

When Iggy arrived at school on Monday morning, he had a daisy in his left hand and invitations to his birthday party in his right hand. He hid the flower in his desk, but Kit Kat got a quick peek as he passed by.

"Who's that for? Mrs. Buff? Suck up," Kit Kat meowed.

"No!" Iggy said, but he stopped to think, *that actually wouldn't be a bad idea.*

Before class started, Iggy placed an invitation on everyone's desk…even Bud's. Iggy knew he couldn't leave anyone out. That would be mean, even if Bud *was* his competition.

"Awesome. You're having your birthday at Future Mountain. The skate park just opened last week," Kit Kat said after ripping open his invitation.

"I've never heard of it," Bud couldn't help but comment.

"Dude, everyone's heard of Future Mountain. It's like the most popular place for kids our age," Snap added.

"What's so cool about it?"

"Can you guys believe this toad? Future Mountain? Man, it's this enormous indoor playground inside the walls of a huge mountain," Snap explained.

Kit Kat jumped in and said, "The inside has an arcade, batting cage, skate park *and* indoor bungee jumps!"

"Don't forget the rock wall and waterslide on the outside of the mountain," Iggy added. "Just wait Bud, you'll love it."

Iggy watched Liz out of the corner of his eye as she walked over to her desk to open her card. A big smile appeared on Liz's face as she read the invitation. "I'll be there," she said as she looked at Iggy.

Iggy took his seat next to Liz and thought about what to say. "How's your arm?"

"Huh? My arm?" she asked, confused.

"Didn't you get a shot on Friday?"

"Oh yeah…you remembered? It's fine, just a little sore," she said and shrugged.

Iggy reached inside his desk and felt the flower's petals with his hand. Liz looked back down at her morning assignments and began working. Iggy felt around for his pencil instead.

That afternoon at recess, Iggy stayed close to Liz. Afraid that Bud might steal her away to go talk, Iggy asked her to climb the big oak tree by the back fence. He knew that Bud couldn't reach her in a tree. It was a brilliant plan.

Iggy and Liz raced to the oak tree. Once the two lizards carefully made their way to the top of the oak, Iggy's palms started to sweat in anticipation.

Liz looked down at his closed fist. "What are you holding?" she asked.

Iggy gulped. It was time. He opened up his shaky hand. The daisy had completely wilted from being in his desk all day, not to mention in his sweaty palm.

"I picked a flower this morning. It was the last one still alive in my mom's flowerbed." Iggy let out a huge sigh.

"Thanks Iggy, that was very nice of you." She peeled back his fingers and took the flower out of his hand, held it to her nose and took a sniff. "Smells like, hmm, smells like…pencil shavings."

"Oh. Well it has been in my desk all day, next to my pencil sharpener," Iggy said smirking.

"I'm sorry, but I don't have anything to give you."

"That's okay, I don't need anything."

Liz smiled.

"Well, I mean if you want to give me something, you can."

"Like what?" Liz asked, still smiling.

Dragon D never told Iggy what to do if the girl he gave a flower to started asking questions. This wasn't exactly what Iggy had planned for. "Um, I mean, I like food."

The two lizards were interrupted by a voice from

the ground. "Hey you guys, we're trying to get teams together for dodge ball. Everyone's been looking for you two."

Iggy looked down to find Bud down at the base of the tree.

"What are you two doing up in that tree?"

"Trying to dodge you," Iggy mumbled under his breath.

"We better go." Liz started to climb down the trunk.

Iggy followed, worried that Liz had no idea why he gave her the flower. Dragon D had said that all he did was give a flower to Darleen and she became his girlfriend. The flower must have been much more impressive than his little wilted daisy. He should have picked a better flower out of his neighbor's flowerbed. It seemed like Liz may be harder to pursue than Iggy thought.

Future
Mountain

On Saturday morning, Iggy was awakened by a fairy princess with a whistle, blowing the happy birthday song softly in his ear. "Good morning your lord, and happy tenth year of life," the little fairy whispered in a creepy, squeaky voice. "Your present awaits you." She pointed her magic wand to a box wrapped in torn out pages from a coloring book.

"Thanks Molly, should I open it now?" Iggy yawned while rubbing his eyes. He could only imagine what was in that tiny little box.

"Yes. Quickly please. Before it dies." Molly leaped off Iggy's bed and grabbed the little box, carefully placing it on the edge of the bed.

133

"Dies? It's alive?"

"Oh," Molly chuckled. "That's just a figure of speech. You'll see if you open it. I picked it out yesterday with Olive."

"But you were at school all day with Little Bit. You got it at school?" Iggy wasn't sure if he even wanted to open it.

"Stop the questions. It's one of a kind." She tapped the box with her wand as if casting a spell.

Iggy pulled the wrapping paper off the raisin box that Molly used to hold her gift. He could hear something making a scratching sound inside. Iggy was kind of afraid to open the box. With curiosity, he slowly peeled back the lid and immediately dropped the box when a huge tree roach came flying toward his face.

"Ahhhhh! What was that? Is it on me?!" Iggy screeched.

Molly rolled around on the ground. "It's just your new pet, Ramon the Roach," she said and laughed.

"You named him?"

"I found him swimming in my grape juice at lunch yesterday. He loves the white grape. I think he's from Spain. Good thing I didn't have purple grape juice or I might have swallowed him!"

"You had a roach in your grape juice? Sick." Iggy shivered with the creeps. Now Ramon the Roach was loose in Iggy's room. Iggy wasn't going to let Ramon ruin his birthday, so he decided to get the day started anyway. Soon he would be meeting his friends at Future Mountain.

Around noon, the whole family, including Dragon D, headed to Future Mountain with Iggy's birthday cake and one big present. On the way, Dragon D whispered to Iggy, "So did it work?"

Iggy knew that he was talking about the flower. "Not exactly," he whispered back, covering the side of his mouth with one hand, so Molly couldn't hear.

"Well, you'll need to go with plan B," Dragon D leaned and whispered into Iggy's ear.

"No secrets!" Molly said pouting.

It didn't matter because Iggy knew what needed

to be done. He had no choice but to ask the obvious question.

Soon the family pulled up to Future Mountain. When Iggy got out of the car and looked up, the mountain seemed even bigger than he remembered.

"Man! This place is huge," Dragon D sighed.

As Iggy and his family approached the door, he saw two pointy, black ears quickly duck down to hide.

"Did you see that?" Iggy asked his cousin.

"See what?"

When Iggy opened the door, all of his friends jumped out and yelled, "SURPRISE!" Molly threw glitter on him.

"Why did everyone hide? I invited you all," Iggy reminded them with a laugh.

Lizibeth ran up to Iggy and gave him a big hug.

Iggy's mom passed out tickets to all of the kids, and everyone ran off in different directions of the mountain. Iggy knew just where he would be going. "Hey, Snap. Want to climb the rock wall?" he asked.

"Dude, have you ever known a turtle to climb, let

alone a wall? I'm keeping my shell on the ground,"
Snap said laughing.

"What was I thinking?" Iggy shrugged.

"I know who you can ask though...maybe that
lizard with the long climbing legs over there." Snap
pointed toward Liz.

"Great idea!" This would give Iggy time to warm
up before he popped the important question. Before
Iggy could get to Liz though, Bud hopped over to her.
She followed him to the batting cage.

"WHAT? This can't be happening," Iggy said and
sighed.

"Come on man, why don't we show that frog who
the real ball players are." Snap headed toward the
batting cages.

"Okay." Iggy followed.

Both reptiles weren't surprised to see Liz pass up
the slow pitch cage and head straight for the fast
pitch. They stood back and watched as she hit every
fastball that was pitched to her. Bud was up to bat
next, but the bullfrog couldn't get one hit.

"Maybe you should try the slow pitch," Liz suggested to Bud.

"No way. That machine is for girls!" Bud yelled sarcastically at Liz.

"Suit yourself." Liz rolled her eyes at the stubborn frog. Right after Bud missed the twelfth throw, Iggy marched his way up to the cage.

"Can I take a hit?" Iggy asked.

"Go ahead. This machine's no good, anyway," Bud grunted and hopped off.

This was Iggy's chance to impress Liz. He hadn't practiced much, but Iggy was great at the fast pitch machine last season. The first pitch came out of nowhere, so he missed. He repositioned himself and breathed out. The ball came toward his bat and he hit it dead on. He hit every one after that.

"That was awesome. I guess Bud was wrong about the machine, huh?" Liz commented.

"Obviously," Iggy said and shrugged.

"So, where should we go next?" she asked.

Iggy knew just where to take Liz. He had been

waiting all week. "How about the rock wall!" Iggy
yelled.

"See you two climbers later," Snap Shell said. "I'll
be on the slides."

Once the lizards arrived to the rock wall, they were
handed two harnesses.

"What are these things for?" Liz asked.

"There're for protection...in case you slip and fall
off the wall," the Future Mountain worker said.

"FALL?" Liz looked worried.

"Don't worry, Liz, it's actually fun to fall. These
ropes are attached to the ceiling, and we can hang
and swing from them," Iggy explained.

Liz and Iggy buckled their harnesses and started up
the wall. Halfway up, Liz lost her grip and fell. The
rope swung back and forth, and she plowed right
into Iggy.

"HELP!" Liz screamed.

Iggy let go to catch Liz and started to swing back and
forth with her. The Future Mountain worker helped
them down once their momentum had stopped.

"I think I need some water," Liz suggested.

"Me too." Iggy figured while he had Liz alone it would be a good time to bring up the question he had on his mind for a while. Once they got to the water fountain, he let her drink first. "Hey Liz?"

"Yeah," she replied after taking a swallow of water.

"I've been meaning to ask you," Iggy froze. The words were stuck in the back of his throat, so he took another way out and asked, "Do you and Bud have a secret?"

"I guess you could say that."

All of a sudden Iggy felt a knot in his stomach and didn't know how to respond.

"Don't look so worried. I think you're misunderstanding me. I shouldn't say anything, but I know why Bud is always angry and so mean."

"You do?"

"Yeah, I think he is really lonely. His parents got a divorce, but neither could take care of him, so Principal Horn adopted him."

"Wow. I had no idea." Iggy was starting to realize

how lucky he was to have such supportive parents.

"No one does. I think he is embarrassed, and if he is anything like his grandpa, you know he's stubborn. I don't really know why he told me. I guess he just needs someone to talk to."

Iggy put all of his jealous feelings aside and tried to put himself in Bud's shoes. "Maybe we could give him another chance," Iggy suggested.

"Well, I do know that he was looking forward to your birthday, even though he never admitted it. He thinks you're pretty cool. We actually talk about you all the time."

Both lizards sat silently for a moment. Iggy wondered what in the world the two of them talked about.

Iggy's mom walked over to tell him that it was time for presents and cake. When Iggy and Liz walked back to the group gathered around all the gifts, he noticed Bud standing alone.

"Hey Liz, do you mind finding the rest of our friends?" Iggy asked.

"Sure." Liz smiled and skipped away.

Iggy knew what he had to do. As he walked over to Bud, a new sense of confidence came over the once bashful lizard. "Bud, I'm glad you got to come to my party. We should try to hang out more."

"We should?" Bud seemed shocked.

"Yeah. Hey, I know how it feels to go to a new school."

Bud stood looking down at his feet. Iggy realized that he had said enough, and he would have to give Bud time. He walked over to his mom who had just lit the candles on his baseball themed cake. As everyone sang, *Happy Birthday*, Iggy watched Bud mouth the words.

Right before Iggy took a breath to blow out his candles, Lizibeth yelled, "Make a wish!"

Iggy responded smiling at Liz, "Already did."

After the entire cake was gone, Iggy's dad brought out a huge box. Molly hopped on top of the box and sat in a meditating position.

Iggy opened up the box, forcing Molly off of it. Inside he found a big blue suitcase. "A suitcase?" Iggy questioned.

"Open up the front zipper, son," Iggy's dad urged him. When Iggy unzipped the top zipper, he found an envelope. He supposed that there would be a card with money inside, but to his surprise, he pulled out two home game tickets to see the Chicago Cubs play... at Wrigley Field!

"Wait a minute," Iggy said, "I'm going to Chicago?"

"Yep. You and me," his dad said. "I'm taking you to the game. I got us tickets right behind the dugout, Champ."

When Iggy actually realized he was going to get to see his favorite team play again on *their* field, he started jumping up and down with excitement.

"You'll find the rest of your present inside the suitcase dear," his mom said.

Iggy unzipped the top flap of the suitcase. Inside, he found a brand new bat and ball.

"Don't forget to take that ball to the game," suggested Snap. "You can definitely get some autographs with those seats."

"You're right!"

That night Iggy pulled out his special shoebox from under his bed with the word, *VALUABLES* written on the top. The game was a month away, so he tucked away the two tickets for safekeeping. He smiled when he laid his new Cubs tickets next to his old ticket stub from five years ago. As the sleepy lizard said his prayers that night, he thanked God for his friends and family. Today, Iggy felt like the luckiest lizard alive.

Will you be my...

February fourteenth was right around the corner, which meant Iggy only had a few days to figure out what he wanted to do for his valentine. His mom found comic strip valentines for him to give to the class, but he knew a comic wasn't going to work for Liz. He needed something special in order to avoid another wilted flower moment.

Iggy snuck into Molly's room to borrow her scissors and glue before she got home from ballet class. He carefully cut out a red heart and glued it to a pink heart which opened up inside. Iggy gathered up the courage to write the words, *Will you be my valentine?* He hid the card inside his valuables box until the big day.

When Friday morning arrived, Iggy reached under his bed to take Liz's valentine out of the box. To his surprise, the box was completely empty, except for one thing...RAMON...belly side up. No valuables, no Cubs tickets and no valentine.

"Molly," Iggy huffed under his breath. He stomped down the hall to his sister's bedroom, but before he could make it all the way down the hall he spotted Liz's valentine. It was taped to the bathroom door. Molly had taken it out of its envelope. Iggy could feel his blood begin to boil. He bolted through her bedroom door, picked up the glass of water she kept on her nightstand and poured it on her face to wake her up.

"SEA MONSTERS!" she screamed.

"It's not a sea monster, you brat! Give me back my Cubs tickets!" Iggy demanded.

"What? I don't have your silly tickets." Molly grinned and started rubbing the water from her eyes.

"Molly, I know you taped that valentine to the door!" Iggy yelled.

"But it was so cute." She batted her eyes.

Meanwhile, all the yelling had woken up Mr. Green. "What is going on in here?" he asked the two lizards.

"Molly took my stuff and messed with...uhhh, some other things, too." Iggy didn't want the whole house to know about his valentine for Liz, but he was fighting back tears of frustration.

"It was just a love note," Molly chimed in.

Iggy rolled his eyes at Molly and stomped back down the hall to his bathroom to take a shower.

When Iggy came downstairs for breakfast, he found all of his stuff neatly piled on his chair at the kitchen table.

"What do you tell your brother, Molly?" Mr. Green crossed his arms and sighed.

"Sorry Iggy. I didn't mean to make you mad." Molly looked like she had been crying.

Iggy had time to cool off, so he replied back, "I know, it's okay."

Molly got up, gave him a hug and darted back

up to her room. It was always hard to stay mad at Molly.

"Is everything okay now?" Iggy's dad asked.

"Yes. I'm ready for school."

"Well, I'm always here to talk if you need me."

"Thanks Dad, but I just want to get to school."

When Iggy walked into class that morning, he found an empty shoebox on his desk. He noticed everyone had a box, so he placed his valentines inside the box and pulled out a spiral notebook from out of his backpack. He looked at the board for the morning assignment. Write *about someone you love.*

Iggy gulped and put his pencil on the first line of a clean sheet of notebook paper.

"Who are you going to write about?" Snap asked as he got comfortable in his chair.

Iggy looked up quickly to find a smirk on Snap's face. "I don't know. Who are you going to write about?"

"My mom, dude. Duh."

"Oh, yeah. Me too." Iggy looked back down and wrote about his mom instead of Liz.

The class rushed through their morning journals, so they could start decorating their shoeboxes with red, white and pink paper and stickers.

At the party, everyone went around the room, dropping a card in each of their classmates' boxes. Iggy had to reseal Liz's card in the same type of envelope as the others, since Molly ruined his original *special* envelope. He dropped her valentine in the box on her desk while she was on the other side of the room.

Once everyone sat back down to open up their cards, Iggy could hear giggling at the back table. He turned around to see what all the commotion was about. A group of girls were gathered around Gwen the Guinea Pig's desk. Out of the corner of Iggy's eye, he could see a valentine that resembled the one he made for Liz. Wait! It WAS the one he made for Liz, but it was in Gwen's pudgy paw.

"I'm going to go over there and see what they are

laughing about," Liz said to Iggy as she got out of her desk.

"Wait…ahhh…NO!" Iggy grabbed for her shoulder.

"I'll be right back. Wait to open your valentine from me until I get back," Liz said as she headed toward the girls' table.

Iggy could only watch in horror as Liz walked away.

"You look flustered. What's wrong man?" Snap asked.

"Just wait, you'll see." Iggy shook his head. When Iggy turned around, he met Liz's eyes. She had a disappointed look on her face.

With a tear in her eye, she walked back to Iggy and said, "I didn't know you liked Gwen. Forget about what I wrote in your card." She grabbed a bathroom pass and ran out of the room.

"Wait, Liz!" Iggy tried to stop her, but she was out the door. He felt a tap on his shoulder and turned around to find the guinea pig standing there, batting her eyelashes.

"Hi!" she said and giggled.

"Uh, hey," Iggy whispered.

"I had no idea." She flashed a big smile at Iggy.

"No," Iggy gulped out. He didn't know what to do.

The guinea pig took his hand, kissed it and scooted back to her seat.

"Yuck!" Iggy spun back around and wiped off his hand.

"Iggy likes Gwen!" Kit Kat cracked up.

"No." Snap Shell shook his head. "That card was for Liz, huh Iggy?"

"Duh!"

"Calm down, I'm just kidding. No need to get your spikes raised."

"What do I do Snap? Liz is crying in the bathroom."

"Open up Liz's card, and see what she wrote to you," suggested Snap.

"Good thinking." Iggy dug through his stack of Valentines. Eventually he came to one in a big red envelope. He figured that had to be the one. When he opened up the card, sure enough, on the front was a picture of him and Liz from his birthday party.

He quickly flipped it open. Inside the card Liz wrote the words,

Iggy dropped the card. He didn't know Liz felt that way about him. LOVE? He reread the card to make sure he wasn't imagining it. He knew he had to fix this mess and fast.

"Go get her, dude. I'll watch for Mrs. Buff."

"Right!" Iggy ran out of the classroom to find Liz, but she was nowhere to be found. He thought about going into the girl's restroom but figured that would get him into a heap of trouble.

In the meantime, Liz had returned back to the class and was sitting quietly at her desk. She saw the opened card on Iggy's desk. Snap Shell watched the lizard take Iggy's valentine back and stuff it in her desk.

"Liz, I don't know why you're upset," Snap said.

"Isn't it obvious?" She looked up and sniffed.

"The whole thing was a mix up, Liz. That card was never intended for Gwen. Somehow it got switched. That card was meant for you."

"You mean to say that Gwen has my valentine?" Liz's eyes got big.

"YES!"

"Where's Iggy?" Liz got up and rushed out of the room.

Iggy showed up moments later with a disappointed look. "She's nowhere to be found," he said mopingly.

"That's because she has been with us this whole time. She just left looking for you. How in the world did you miss her?" Snap threw his hands in the air.

"I don't know. Maybe she went around the corner by our lockers," Iggy said.

"Well, if I were you, I would get that valentine back from your pig," suggested the cat.

"You're right." Iggy bravely walked over to Gwen. "Um, Gwen?" He tapped her on the shoulder.

"Iggy! What a pleasant surprise," she said while batting her eyes, again and again and again.

"Please stop batting your eyes, it's kind of creepy." Iggy couldn't concentrate. "So about the valentine."

"Yes, it was lovely," she said and smiled. "I wish I had something special for you."

"Um, yeah, so about that. I meant to give it to someone else." Iggy bit his lip in anticipation of her reaction.

"WHAT? WHO?" the pig squealed.

"It's for Liz. The card is for Liz," croaked a voice from behind.

Iggy turned around to see Bud and Liz standing behind him. Bud had found Liz in the hall and brought her back to Iggy.

"Fine! You're not my type anyway." Gwen threw the card in Iggy's face and ran away.

"I didn't mean to upset you." Iggy couldn't believe what a mess this had become. But right now all that mattered was Liz. The green iguana turned around to give the valentine to the right animal and Liz's cheeks started to turn a bright shade of pink. After she opened the card and read the words for the second time, she wrapped her arms around Iggy and gave him a big hug.

The whole class started to clap and scream, "WOOHOO, YEAH!!!!"

"Dude! You're the man!" Snap was so proud. "You never once changed colors."

Iggy realized that Snap was right. He had stayed green through all the turmoil of the day.

Later that night at the dinner table, the phone rang. Molly darted from her chair to grab it. "It's probably for me. Olive always calls at this hour. Hello. Yes, he's here, but he's eating his broccoli right now."

"Molly, just give it to me." Iggy grabbed the phone.

"Son, be quick. We're eating," said his dad.

"Hello?"

"Hi, Iggy. Sorry to call in the middle of dinnertime, but I forgot to tell you yes."

"Yes?" he questioned.

"You know. Yes. I'll be your girlfriend. I mean valentine."

"Oh, thanks, that's...that's awesome! Can I call you after dinner?"

"Sure!"

Iggy hung up and walked back to his seat.

"Who was that dear?" asked his mom.

With a proud and confident grin on his face, Iggy replied, "Just my girlfriend."

The
End

What's Next?

Can't wait to see what happens next?
Look out for Iggy the Iguana's summer
vacation story, *Summer League*. Turn the
page for a sneak peek! Be sure to keep
up with Iggy's news at his website:

www.Iggytheiguana.com

From Book #2 in the Iggy the Iguana Series

Summer League

Iggy shook his head trying to get his focus back on his destination, the mound. "Just get through this game," he told himself. They had to beat the Bear Dogs to get to District.

The Bear Dogs were first up to bat. Iggy stood on the pitcher's mound, eying the big brown rat in the batter's box wiggling his bat over his shoulder. Iggy was about to spit to intimidate the rat, but then saw Liz watching him from the bleachers and decided to hold back. Iggy could hear Snap snort and watched the turtle drop down one finger. Iggy nodded, signaling the heat. As the lizard's left leg raised to wind up for the pitch, he cringed and accelerated to throw a fastball to the rat. To Iggy's surprise, the rat hit the ball and made it to 3rd base on the first pitch and with rodent speed. A triple.

The Star's catcher noticed the look on his pitcher's face and called a time-out. When Snap approached Iggy on the rubber he asked, "Dude? You hurt?"

"It's cool, it's cool. Just tight."

Snap looked at Iggy through his mask, trying to get the truth out of him. "You better not be lying to me, bro." Snap turned his head to spit out a sunflower shell.

Iggy nodded and tugged at his cap.

By the bottom of the fifth inning the Bear Dogs were ahead by one point. Digger called a meeting at the mound. Marc the Mouse was on first base and Cooper was up to bat. Iggy hoped the chameleon would hit it to the rattlesnake who wasn't very good with handling the ball.

Digger threw the ball and Cooper hit it straight toward the snake. Marc headed to second base as

Coop took first. Buddy hopped up to the plate and decided to also take advantage of the Bear Dog's weakest link. Buddy hit it in the rattler's direction but only advanced each runner one base. Now, the bases were loaded and Iggy needed to clean the bases. This was his chance for a grand slam, and guarantee their spot in the District Tournament.

Iggy grabbed his helmet and strutted to the batter's box. He dug his right foot in the dirt, twisting the ball of his foot back and forth in the batter's box. When his left foot was set, Iggy held the bat high above his right shoulder. Pain started at his elbow and gradually trickled down into his forearm. He heard a voice in his head telling him to call a time out. *Don't do it Iggy.* The voice kept repeating. *You'll get hurt this time.* The same voice then started to say, *Just one more swing. You're about to win the game.* His conscience wouldn't stop. *Don't do it Iggy. Just one more swing. Don't do it. Just one more.* Iggy shook the voices out of his head and he reminded himself to breath as he saw Digger mouth something under his breath. He knew Digger could have any type of pitch up his sleeve. Iggy was ready for anything: slow ball, curveball, knuckleball, or even Digger's heater, his hard-to-hit fastball. Iggy could feel time go still, zoning out the yells and heckles in the crowd. Iggy gripped the bat and stared Digger right in the eyes.

Digger hid the ball behind his right leg, toying with the ball in his hand, set back and threw the hardest, fastball the lizard had ever seen.

Iggy swung the bat and the ball flew like a rocket across the field. All of the players on base took off. Marc jogged in for the tying run. Cooper followed him, giving the Stars a one run advantage. Buddy hurriedly hopped to home plate putting them ahead by two.

Iggy fell to his knees on first and grasped his arm. He couldn't make it any farther. He dropped his head and tried to catch his breath. The base umpire called time out and Coach Brown and Coach Green ran toward first.

About the Author

~ ★ ~

MELISSA M. WILLIAMS is the author of the *Iggy the Iguana* chapter book series, the *Turtle Town* chapter book series and the *Little Miss Molly* picture book for kids, the owner of LongTale Publishing and founder of the Literacy Non-Profit Organization—READ3Zero. Born and raised in Houston, Texas, Melissa has been writing stories since she was a little girl and still uses that childhood love for imagination to relate

to her young readers today. During graduate school, Melissa began substitute teaching for elementary grades in order to learn from her students. She received a Master's degree in professional counseling and implements psychological skills when presenting to her young audiences. After speaking to thousands of students and teachers at over two hundred schools across Texas and California, she expanded her instruction in order to share specific creative techniques with educators. Melissa's main focus today revolves around recognizing the need to keep reading, writing and creativity inside the home and classroom while balancing electronic usage. Her literacy organization hosts the *I Write Short Stories by Kids for Kids* Publishing Contest, offering opportunities for children to become published authors, illustrators and speakers.

More information can be found at
www.MelissaMWilliamsAuthor.com

The Real Iggy

~ ★ ~

In third grade, I got my first pet for making the honor roll. I had no interest in getting a puppy, kitty, or hamster...because I loved reptiles! My dad used to bring home huge field lizards in the summertime, and on the weekends, we would go out to the bayou to catch turtles. When we got to the pet store, I headed straight to the reptile section. Iggy was the cutest iguana in the whole aquarium! As a baby iguana, he had the most beautiful pastel scales. I took Iggy home and treated him as if he were my very own baby. Iggy had birthday parties, school lessons, his own shirts and ties that I had sewn myself, a miniature backpack, hats and his own pillow. By the time Iggy was two years old, he could sit up on his hind legs for his favorite treat, bananas. He was even potty-trained. When Iggy outgrew his aquarium, the three-foot-long lizard lived on top of my bookshelf. He had a carpeted ramp to walk down when he needed to go to the bathroom. He would wait by the back door to be let outside, just like a dog. Everyday when I got home from school, I would take him in the backyard to work on his suntan while I did my homework in the grass.

Iggy was a huge responsibility for me. He liked getting attention and expected playtime each day. He loved to

Melissa age 8 and Iggy the Green Iguana

exercise, and I had to be careful because if Iggy spotted a good-looking tree, he would head over to climb it. One day, I accidentally left Iggy outside, and I thought he was lost forever! After an hour of searching for him with my family, my dad spotted him in the highest part of our neighbor's tree. We had to get a ladder to get him down. Boy was I relieved. Iggy was like a best friend to me. As a little girl, I loved to write. I had a huge imagination! I would write stories about Iggy and his best friend, Snap Shell. Throughout the years, I had many different iguanas, horned toads and turtles as pets, and many of my pets are main characters in the *Iggy the Iguana* story. Some of my best memories were my adventures with Iggy. Now his memory will live on in the chapters of the *Iggy the Iguana* books.

Acknowledgments

∾ ★ ∾

I am so thrilled to share this second edition of the first book in the *Iggy the Iguana* Series. Thank you to our creative team; many who have been there since the very beginning. It has been so exciting to see my illustrator, Kelley Ryan's new renditions of the characters. I still remember the very first sketch of Iggy back in 2007. Sharon Wilkerson has been there since the beginning as well, through the long nights of edits and revisions. I couldn't do any of this without you. It's been so much fun to work with Monica Thomas and Tamara Dever at TLC Graphics. Your creativity blows me away. Sue Kinane, you are my second brain, helping me keep all my business endeavors together. I'm so thankful for the love and support of my family. As always, I thank God as He continues to bless these visions and the work I do with children. They are the future. I hope to always encourage kids to read and use their imagination. Last but not least, thank you to all of the readers who give me a reason to write these stories. When I write, I'm always thinking about you.

Books by Melissa M. Williams

New School, New Rules
Book 1 of Iggy the Iguana Series
Ages 7-11
168 pages
5½ x 8½ paperback or hardcover

Summer League
Book 2 of Iggy the Iguana Series
Ages 7-11
210 pages
5½ x 8½ paperback or hardcover

Crazy Days of 5th Grade
Book 3 of Iggy the Iguana Series
Ages 7-11
230 pages
5½ x 8½ paperback or hardcover

Books are available at
IggytheIguana.com
TurtleTown.com
LittleMissMollyBooks.com

Also available at
BarnesandNoble.com
and Amazon.com

For information
about author school
visits, creative writing
workshops, and public
speaking requests, e-mail
Melissa@LongTale
Publishing.com
or visit
MelissaMWilliamsAuthor.com

The Inner Puka
Book 1 of Turtle Town Series
Ages 8-12
240 pages
5½ x 8½ paperback

The Green Room
Book 2 of Turtle Town Series
Ages 8-12
264 pages
5½ x 8½ paperback

Houston, Texas

Little Miss Molly
Children's picture book
Ages 3-8
32 pages
10 x 10 hardcover

Little Miss Molly
Coloring book
Ages 3 and up
32 pages
8 x 10 paperback